SAMMY TRIES HORSEBREAKING

They were nearing the fence again. Sammy hauled on the bridle, throwing her weight, and pulled sideways. She had to get him leveled out, send him into a circling run away from the barrier. But it was no good.

He was past responding to the steel in his mouth, past veering away from an obstacle. He must have been aware only of the hateful presence on his back.

Up he went, his front feet clearing the bars, but he had leaped too near his hurdle, and Sammy's frantic pressure on the bit impeded the jump. They struck the fence with a rending crash . . .

PROMISE OF TOMORROW

Jeanne Williams

for SARITA
whose Magic Hand
has eased
much pain for many

CHAPTER ONE

In the last flush of sunset Sammy Forrester saw a *vaquero* etched black against the sky. She stopped her bay mare, Chispa, by a mesquite and watched to see what the man was doing. He held his peaked sombrero before him on the saddle horn and his horse cropped the grass as the rider stared at the lake—a lake that spread where none used to be, a lake that covered the old village, flowed over the church, the streets where children had shouted and played for two hundred years till the building of Falcón, the great dam forty miles southeast down the Rio Grande.

Recognizing the man as Diego Ruiz, Sammy started to wave and call, then decided not to. Perhaps Diego had things to say to the red sundown and his lost home. He had been the last person to leave Zapata. Bitterly, he had brought up the gravestones of his mother, father, and grandparents, placing them in the cemetery by the new Zapata, which was filled with refugees from the drowned village.

That had been six years ago, in 1953, but Diego didn't seem to be able to forget. Saddened for him and the old town, Sammy looped Chispa about and took the trail home. Whit was coming tonight. It would be the last time she'd see him before he went back to A & M for the fall term.

Miss a minute of this last evening? Not if she could help it! Since she had come to Texas four years ago, there hadn't been anyone for her but Whit Granger. In a bigger school he probably wouldn't have noticed her, he a senior, she a lowly frosh. But El Sauz Consolidated High School, with a total enrollment of fifty-nine, had few age or class divisions. She had been afraid that after Whit left for college he'd meet some girl from Baylor or Texas University, but instead he had asked her up for dances and ball games, dated her in the summers; and now she was through high school and he was a senior, with the spurs, riding boots, and sword that members of the A & M Corps of Cadets wore for dress occasions their last year.

What was the special thing Whit wanted to tell her this evening? Laughing in anticipation, Sammy urged Chispa on faster, for she was sure she knew. Whit was going to ask her to be engaged!

There was nothing else that could merit the sober way he'd announced on the phone that he had something important to talk over. She had always been Whit's girl. It seemed the only right and natural thing for them to marry, live here at Los Ladinos, and raise fine horses. Sammy whistled and laughed with sheer happiness as she crossed the highway and took the gravel road that led to Uncle Voss' ranch.

This first week of September looked no different from August in the brushlands. Gray-silver sage was in purple bloom, the *retama's* frondy boughs held bursts of yellow blossoms, and huge clumps of prickly-pear cactus were topped with the maroon *tunas,* oval and spined with needles, which were fed to cattle after the spines were seared off with flame throwers. This was raw, harsh country with thorns on almost every plant and water an eternal problem, but Sammy loved it. For it was also a golden world where time seemed to have fallen asleep; where the soft Spanish tongue was heard more often than English; where the *vaqueros* wore their leather clothes, and Martín, foreman of the Los Ladinos men, rolled his cornshuck cigarettes and mounted his horse while saying the old prayer-formula, *"En el Nombre de Dios,"* in the Name of God.

Sammy loved, too, the gate before which she now dismounted. It was made of wrought iron and each half was fastened to a stone pillar. A niche was carved in both pillars about waist-high, and on one small shelf stood Mexico's Madonna, the Virgin of Guadalupe. The other shelf held a wooden image of San Isidro, the name saint of the Spaniard who had founded the ranch and given it the name that twined ornately over the iron gate: *San Isidro de Los Ladinos.*

"Saint Isidro of the Wild Ones." The Spaniard had named it rightly, for it had become a great horse ranch spread over miles of unfenced brushland. *Vaqueros* rode in vast circles, bringing in the mustangs, the wild horses.

The best of these had been saved to breed until the horses of Los Ladinos became known throughout the Border. Tough, gamy little beasts, they endured the cruel thorns as gallantly as their Barb and Arab ancestors had paced the fierce Arabian deserts. But the Spaniard died and his heirs had no taste for this ranch in the middle of nowhere. They sold out, a hundred years ago, and later owners let it fall away from its pride, selling off the horses and keeping it only as grazing land.

Uncle Voss bought it after his forced retirement from the Army because of wounds received in World War II. Because of his health, he concentrated on farming, growing watermelons; but Sammy dreamed of a time when Los Ladinos horses would be famous again.

She led Chispa through the gate, closed it with a good-by smile at the *santos,* and rode down the mile-long, tamarisk-shaded lane to the house.

Martín and the other two *vaqueros,* Vicente and Jorge, were unsaddling in the mesquite-limb corral when she rode up. Martín, hurrying, was the first to open the gate.

"Señorita Sam!" He used the teasing, affectionate name she was called by. "You should have been with us today. We branded the last of the yearlings out north in the brush corrals. And we saw a coyote dun!"

"What's that?" Sammy puzzled, stepping down from the saddle.

Martín's steel-gray brows pulled together. He surveyed her in astonishment as he loosened the cinch, yanked off the saddle and blanket, removed the bridle, and sent Chispa off toward the watering tank. Pushing back his grizzled hair, the chief *vaquero* explained:

"You fit Los Ladinos so truly that I forget you grew up far from here and do not understand all our things. A coyote dun is a horse the yellow-gray shade of a coyote, and bears down his spine the black markings that mean wildness. It is said a coyote dun will drop in his tracks before failing his rider."

Jorge Gonzales, Martín's black-haired grandson, laughed over his shoulder as he hung his saddle on the fence. "Without doubt that is true. But becoming the rider—that is the problem!"

"Is the horse ours?" Sammy asked, intrigued with this talk.

"He's on Los Ladinos graze and none of the neighbors have duns." Martín turned to Vicente Montes who was the best man with horses in all the county. Vicente's great-grandfather had been a Comanche chief who got his Mexican wife during one of the Border raids, and the blood of that tribe of incomparable horsemen showed in his broad cheekbones as well as his riding. To him, horses had more personality than people, and he never forgot one. So Martín questioned him.

"Do you remember the dun mare who disappeared two years ago at about the time she was to foal?"

Vicente nodded. "That was Mesteña. She had never been broken. We didn't find her colt, but I found a hide and bones that looked like hers up near Tigre Creek last summer. It is probable that the coyote dun we saw today was her foal."

"But how come no one ever saw him before?" Sammy asked.

Old Martín shrugged. "Ay, Señorita Sam, you know the country north up in the little hills. Thickets of thorn and cactus. We only go there in the fall to brand the calves."

"It was luck, simply, that we saw the horse at all," said Jorge. "He was running along the top of that bare hill we call the *Peloncillo* because it looks like a sugar loaf. My horse whinnied and the wild one froze. He stood there— like a statue, Señorita Sam! Then he plunged and sped out of sight."

Sammy glanced north toward the dim, jagged line of small hills. "I wish I'd seen him," she said wistfully. "He sounds like a real mustang. The kind they used to raise on Los Ladinos."

"He may be," Vicente mused. "His mother, if indeed he's Mesteña's son, was one of the last of the old Ladinos breed, *puro español.*"

Before Sammy could ask if the wild horse couldn't be tamed, a long-drawn-out *bbeee-e-ep!* set the hair prickling at the back of her neck and stampeded the horses through the corral gate into the pasture.

"You certainly let people know you're coming!" Sammy cried as she whirled to confront the grinning redhead at the wheel of the jeep. Only Chuck, her twin brother, made such a racket.

"I wouldn't want anyone to miss me," he laughed, coming off the seat and flipping Sammy with the wet towel that told he'd been swimming at the reservoir. Sammy hated water outside of a shower or a drinking glass.

"Don't do that!" she squealed.

"Why not? A scorcher like today, and instead of cheering your poor brother's last day at home, you go riding!"

"You swim and I'll ride," Sammy retorted. "It's time you went to A & M. From what Whit says about the Cadets Corps, it'll straighten you out!"

With a wink at Martín, Chuck said, "Shucks, I'm fixin' to revolutionize it. After all, I'm fourth-generation Forrester at the dear old school."

"I have a word for you—Fish Forrester will be just another freshman! If you're smart, you'll swim underwater with the other fish and ignore the baits of upperclassmen." Fish was the name given to freshmen in the Corps. Having properly squelched her twin, Sammy glanced at her watch.

"Seven o'clock!" she shrieked. "Whit'll be here in thirty minutes. Chuck, be an angel! Rub Chispa down and give her some grain?"

He groaned but untwined his long legs and slipped into the corral. "I should know better than come around you when you're lookin' for old Whit. Well, go on and get pretty."

Sammy ran toward the house a quarter-mile away.

Shaded by tamarisks, giant mesquites, banana trees, and royal palms, the cream-plastered adobe house had been built by old Don Isidro. A veranda ran the length of the front, furnished with comfortable, if shabby, wicker chairs, and Mexican ollas planted with geraniums and marigolds.

U-shaped, the house folded around a patio, and as Sammy passed through the huge living room and entered the hall that opened into the other rooms from off the patio, she heard Martín's youngest grandson, Tomás, singing in his shrill, sweet voice as he trimmed the bougainvillaeas. She mentally translated the song:

> "If someday you pass by my house,
> Do not forget ever that I was your lover.
> Because anyway, in the world there are other lovers.
> As I loved you, so can I forget you."

"*Hola,* old one!" Sammy laughed, bobbing through the arched portal. "With whom are you in love now?"

Eleven-year-old Tomás grinned. He snipped off a crimson hibiscus, tossed it through the arch. His black eyes sparkled with fun.

"Only with you, Señorita Sam!"

Tucking the flower behind her ear, she swept a low curtsy to answer his bow. "Thousand thanks, *Señor!*" She waved and rushed along to her room.

Goodness, she shouldn't have been playing! She had to shower, and Guadalupe should have help getting the meal ready. This would have to be a quick trick. Wasn't it lucky that Whit always liked the way she looked?

Exactly twenty minutes later she took a final check in the mirror as she thrust her feet into thong sandals. She wore the plain white dress with its straw belt that Whit liked so much, lipstick that flattered the gold tones of her skin, and a white *piqué* headband that caught back her black hair, which the sun had touched to auburn in places. Perfume from the bottle, ridiculously large because Chuck had bought it in Mexico where prices were low, finished Sammy's dressing.

Even in her hurry to get to the kitchen, she paused in the hall a moment to smile at the large wooden figure of San Isidro which had guarded the end of the hall for over a century. Above her head, the ceiling of small saplings plastered together with clay made a herringbone pattern, and beyond the thick arches opening to the patio bloomed garish wine-colored bougainvillaea, and the hibiscus she loved better than any other flower—oh, white walls, the bitter-pleasant smell of the salt cedar, and the flowers so lovely it hurt. She could live here forever. Never want another place, another home.

Here it was easy to slip back to an ancient time and graciousness, forget the world of planes and highways and noise. This sunny, golden world had roots that went deep, it wouldn't change. Maybe that was one reason she loved it.

For she had never had a place with dreams before. She had lived the drifting life of the Air Force, never in one town more than a few years, barely getting used to it before it was time to leave. She learned the hard way not to like friends or school or a place too well so that it wouldn't hurt so much to lose them. But always she wanted to have a home and belong somewhere. When she heard her classmates talk about things they had done back in first grade, she felt as if a door banged in her face, shutting her out.

Still, there was Chuck, and having a twin was a very special thing. They even had "twin twinges," when things happened to one of them, and could sometimes tell exactly what the absent one was thinking.

Most of all, there were Dad and Mother. Dad, the picture of a career officer, tall and dark, with eyes that matched the dark blue of the winter uniform, and Mother, tiny and slender, with red-gold hair. Parents like them made a world, no matter where you were. Their love, laughter, and courage had made living in that old waterfront house in Virginia seem gay and adventurous, turned the boiled-cabbage smell of the factory near Houston into a shared joke, made the heat of Panama endurable, even made private rental in Japan exciting fun rather than a pain in the neck. When Dad had flown combat tours in Korea and Europe, Mother had somehow still kept them all united.

The Air Force was their life, and it had some good points. Usually there were a few other Air Force kids in school, and besides, the home-town crowd seemed to think it was glamorous and wanted to be friends. As long as the family were together, it was fine.

Then, three years ago, when the twins had been sophomores, Dad got orders for Labrador. They stayed in school but Mother, wanting to be with Dad as long as possible, had driven him to New York. Slick roads, a sharp curve— a skid, and that was it. Dad and Mother, gone together, gone for good.

Uncle Voss, Dad's older brother, had taken the twins out of their crashed world, back to his ranch. It had been a blessing to find a life so different because there was less to remind them of their parents, it was easier to start fresh.

Now, as Sammy ran down the hall, she drew deep breaths of the tangy air, glowingly happy because Whit loved the brush country too. He wouldn't want to go away from this place she had become a part of. Oh, of course, he was taking the flying program at A & M. He'd have to serve a few years as a pilot, but then he'd come back here. Together, they could make Los Ladinos famous again for its horses.

Voices floated out of the kitchen. ". . . the fine *enchi-*

ladas Wheet likes," Guadalupe was saying, "and some *leche dulce.*"

"Whit!" snorted Chuck. "Don't you care about what I like, Lupe?"

"Yes, but you eat anything whatever," Guadalupe sniffed, briskly shredding lettuce for *tacos.* "Just like Sammy-*Mula!*"

"I heard that!" Sammy objected, giving the plump, aging woman a hug. "Who could help eating the good things you make? Here, let me fix the *tacos.* Chuck, be useful and set the table."

He took an armload of plates and silver. His whistling echoed back from the dining room and Sammy trilled along with him. Lupe clucked disapprovingly.

"Whistling girls and crowing hens, Sammy-*Mula!*" Lupe had made that name up from Samuela, Sammy's real name, and *mula,* the Spanish word for mule, because she thought Sammy often behaved like one. "Some night you'll whistle up an *onza.*"

"What's that?" asked Sammy, deftly wrapping *tortillas* about the shredded lettuce, tomatoes, peppers, and meat sauce that form the stuffing for *tacos.*

"An *onza* has green eyes," Lupe said darkly, shaking her finger. "It looks like a cat but it's really a bad human with the power to change form. It eats things——"

"And if there's one thing you think it ought to gobble, it's a whistling girl!" Sammy finished, chuckling.

"It isn't just the whistling," Lupe retorted. "A proper young lady—who wishes to marry—does not ride horses all day and act as if she would never grow up." Her head jerked up and down emphatically. "You must mend your ways, Sammy-*Mula,* if you want Wheet."

Sammy kissed her old friend's cheek. "Don't worry, Lupe. I don't think my whistling will scare Whit. In fact, I sort of think he may——" She broke off at the sound of tires crunching down the road. Lupe gave her a push.

"That's Wheet! Go meet him before you spill chili on your dress! I can get the meal on now."

She didn't wait for him to get out of his father's pickup. Heart racing, she ran down the steps, was stopped by strong brown hands that gripped her wrists and brought her close for a kiss.

"Sammy!" He put her back to look at her with the blue

eyes that smiled out of a tanned, square-jawed face. Already topping six feet, Whit wasn't handsome, rather rangy, but he moved with a quiet assurance that made him stand out in any crowd. He tucked her arm through his.

"Darn," he said ruefully as they walked to the house. "I barely got home from summer ROTC training and I have to go again! I wish Los Ladinos were a few hundred miles nearer to College Station."

"That is a problem," Sammy agreed. Was he going to say it now? The important thing?

She glanced up. There was an odd, strained look to his mouth and eyes that vanished in a grin as he rushed her up the steps.

"Come on, Sammy! I smell *enchiladas* and *leche dulce.*" She tried to smother a stab of misgiving. It was natural for a man about to propose to be nervous, wasn't it? But why had he cut off her chance to ask what was wrong?

Shrugging, she took the hostess' place at the table. His hands, catching her close to him, had said he loved her. Surely any other problem could be worked out.

CHAPTER TWO

Doodlebug came in, late as usual, hung his peach twig by the mantel, and joined them after washing. He was a white-haired old man who had worked in the early oil fields. Several years ago Sammy had found him 'way off in the little hills, lost and without water, but sure his peach twig had located oil. Since then, he had lived at Los Ladinos, helping with the work and scouting the country for one last gusher that would make him rich.

"Sorry to drag in like this," he apologized, pulling up a heavy leather chair. "I found a place on Tigre Creek that just felt like there *had* to be oil but I couldn't find a thing. Doggone it!"

"I know how you feel," said Uncle Voss from the other end of the table. Thin as a string bean, burned saddle-brown from wind and sun, he had the outdoorsman's crow's-feet around his gray eyes that came from peering across the white land to the brazen sky. "I thought last night I'd man-

aged to call up old Loney, durned melon-eater that she is!
She sang back at me awhile and I was getting up to where I
could aim when—whoosh! Off like a jack rabbit's ghost."
He slapped his hands past each other to demonstrate and
sighed.

"I keep telling you, Uncle Voss," said Chuck. "You won't
catch that old coyote unless you put out traps or poison."

"Don't like to do that, son. I'm not after coyotes in general any more than the police are after people in general
when they hunt a killer. Coyotes keep the jack rabbits down
and catch a lot of pesky bugs. Poison and traps catch badger
and quail and even deer and calves. Except when some real
pesky thief like Loney plagues around, I like to let nature
balance the wildlife."

Piling beans and meat on his fork as businesslike as if he
were stocking a fire engine, Doodlebug spoke up:

"Folks don't much believe in leaving things to nature any
more. Look what they've done to the oil fields! Used to be
some fun in it, some gambling to get your blood high. Now
they make test holes and hire geologists and study maps
till it's no wonder the dicky bird won't sing for 'em." He
took a great draught of coffee. "Praise be, I remember Spindletop, Burkburnett, and Tampico—back when roughnecks were rough and drillers drilled and geologists minded
their cotton-pickin' business!"

"What is a dicky bird?" asked Sammy. She wished Whit
would look at her. The *enchiladas* weren't that marvelous!

Doodlebug neatly cleaned chili sauce off his white mus-
tache before he answered: "Why, Miss Sam, haven't I told
you? He's a great creature with cast-iron feathers and a
squawk like the walking beam of a derrick. When he'd sing
to a man, that fella had to drop everything and go hunt for
oil." Doodlebug sighed. "I heard him, before I went to
Spindletop. But he's gone away for good now. Oil men don't
pay attention to peach twigs or dicky birds. Not a driller left
with any kind of nerve. They're *business*men."

"Ouch!" Chuck laughed, winking at Uncle Voss. "Bet
that's how Martín feels every time he rides by those watermelons in the east pasture. What kind of ranchers is he
working for?"

Uncle Voss smiled ruefully but didn't answer. Sammy
took up the challenge. "There's no reason why this can't
be a famous horse ranch again. We could try breeding back

to a mustang type, fast and tough for ranch use. Martín even saw a coyote dun on our range! Maybe we could catch him to begin. We would make another great Los Ladinos line."

"That'd be a life's work," Uncle Voss said. "I just retired here to keep busy and pay expenses, honey, not compete with old Don Isidro."

"Oh, but——" Sammy whirled urgently to Whit. "You want to raise horses, don't you, Whit? Not as a side line or hobby, but as a serious thing?" They used to talk about it, read the horse magazines, and follow sales. But as Whit stared at his plate, Sammy remembered that he hadn't mentioned it for a long time. A year at least now that she stopped to think . . .

His tone was expressionless. "Haven't you forgotten I have to go into the Air Force, Sammy?"

"Only for three years. After that——"

His head came up and he tucked his chin under in the military manner he assumed when he had an unpleasant chore. "It's not just for three years. That ruling has changed. If a man wants to take the flight training in ROTC and be commissioned a flying officer, he has to agree to stay in for five years."

And Whit wanted to fly. Sammy stared at him, not daring to press him further in front of the others. Five years? Why, if he stayed in that long, he might stay in for life! She knew in another minute the tears would come. Hastily stumbling to her feet, she murmured an apology and fled down the hall toward her room, vainly trying to blink her eyes free of the hot, bitter stinging. Whit hadn't decided this in a hurry. He never acted on impulse. How long had he listened to her babble on about her plans for the ranch while he knew he wasn't coming back after three years, as she had confidently expected?

"Sammy!" His long legs caught up with her. "I was going to tell you tonight. Only not like that."

Hating her chin for quivering, she wouldn't look at him. "I—oh, Whit, how long have you known this?"

"I signed the contract last year."

And didn't tell me? "I just can't believe it," she said, struggling to control herself. "I always thought——" She broke off. Tell him what she had hoped for tonight? Reproach or blame him? No, she wouldn't do that, not if she bit her tongue out. He turned her to the patio.

"Let's sit down out here and talk this over, Sammy."

"I don't—feel like it."

"I'm sorry about the way I had to blurt it out. But I've been thinking. Hard. And we need to talk before I leave in the morning. Please, Sammy?"

The touch of his hand pleaded silently. This wasn't easy for him, she realized, and in spite of the hurt in her heart, she didn't want to make it harder for him.

"All right." She sat down on one of the stone benches. "Fire away." Her choice of words had been unconscious but he flinched.

"Look, I'm not a firing squad. But I can't go to school and leave—well, *us,* up in the air. I didn't just sign for five years. I want to make flying my career."

The pain inside her twisted, sank all the way through her numbed feelings. Not three years in the Air Force then— not five, but his whole life. She folded her fingers sharply into her palms, but managed to speak in a level voice:

"I suppose you're sure about that, Whit?"

He nodded. "I've been over and over it ever since I signed that contract. I love flying, Sammy. I like the military. But we—well, we've gone steady and I know I sort of took it for granted that we'd get married someday. Of course I know how much you want to stay on the ranch and it is a good life except—please try to understand! I've found what I really want. If I didn't do it, I wouldn't be satisfied with anything else."

"A person ought to want to do what he picks for his work and life," Sammy agreed slowly. *Only what about me? Don't I have any choice?* As if he read her mind, Whit took her hand and held it between his big, lean ones as he had done so often.

"I guess it doesn't seem fair for a man to pick his job and leave the girl only the choice of playing along or looking for someone else. That's the way it is, though. And things, including us, have changed in the last few years. Maybe I've noticed it more because I'm older and I've been away. Before we think about marriage we have to be sure we're in love for keeps. Enough for you to accept my work, and I know that would be mighty hard."

"Are you trying to say you don't love me, Whit?"

"Good grief, no!" He scrubbed back his crew cut in irritation. "I love you and you must love me or you'd have run me off long ago. But especially with me going into the Air Force, we have to find out just how we do feel about each other. I'm asking you to do this, Sammy, in order to give us time to think. Go out with other fellows this year. Act as if I didn't exist."

She stared at him in shock. With an exasperated breath he took her face between his hands and kissed her.

"Sammy, quit thinking I'm giving you the run-around! That's exactly what I don't want to do! I want you to be happy and I may not be the guy to do it if I take you away from Los Ladinos. Roam wild and free till next spring or summer and then we'll see how you feel. You may be engaged to some rich cattleman by then."

Sammy could scarcely resist saying, *Do you hope I will?* But that was mean. Whit was trying to do the best thing for her; why didn't he see that it was wounding, humiliating, to have him tell her to play the field on the night she had expected an engagement ring?

"You mean we won't date this winter?"

"I think it'd be a way of seeing if this is the real thing or a nice habit. Darn, honey, you've gone with me since you were fourteen! Get somebody to compare me with, and you may wonder what you ever saw in me." Holding her eyes, he said commandingly, "Put me out of your mind all you can. Don't write. Have a ball. If by, oh, say about Ring Dance time, you think you could take the Air Force, we'll talk it over."

The Ring Dance, held near the end of the school year, was the big senior event when the cadets' best girls turned the seniors' till-now-reversed class rings, right way up. It seemed forever until then. Fall, winter, spring. Sammy looked ahead, feeling the days spiral down on her like smothering dead leaves. Like a wounded animal, she wanted to get away and hide.

She stood up. "Then this is so long for a while, Whit. *Vaya con Dios.* And—thanks for being honest." Before he could stop her, she moved quickly toward her room. She hadn't made a show, she didn't want to, but she had to get this crushing weight off her chest.

In her room, she ran to the big window carved out of the thick adobe, gripped the cool iron grillwork, and wept.

After the first tempest she began to think. While she'd
been absorbed in her dreams of the ranch and a new line of
horses, Whit had moved on to look at the sky and the outside world she distrusted. It boiled down to this: he was
taking the Air Force even if it meant giving her up. Could
he really love her?

Furrowing her brow, thinking of her father and Uncle
Voss, she had to admit he could. A man's work was somehow more important to him, in a different way, than his
family. When a girl married, her work was making a home
and caring for her family. That had to be enough to make
up for a location or job she didn't like.

If Whit had asked me tonight to marry him, Air Force
and all, what would I have said? she wondered.

Now there was a question! And she didn't know, search
herself as she might. Give up her long dream of Los Ladinos
for little yards and project housing, the separations and
overseas tours she remembered all too vividly?

Whit was right. They had to be very sure. Still, it was so
long till the Ring Dance! Far up through the months flickered a small candle of hope. Whit would be thinking too.
Knowing what the ranch meant to her, mightn't he think of
some compromise? She pressed her cheek against the grillwork, but neither it nor the east wind carried any healing.
This was growing up: facing unalterable facts and deciding
if you could change while you hurt, as if you were physically
being pulled and kneaded and stretched into a new shape.

Whit's pickup had ground off long ago. She washed her
face and went to help Guadalupe with the dishes.

She caught a quick little breath of relief when Uncle Voss
and Doodlebug weren't in sight. As she stepped into the
kitchen, Lupe glanced up from the sink and clucked sadly. It
was Chuck, polishing glasses, who spoke:

"You and ole Whit have a fight?"

"Certainly not!"

"Then why did he leave so fast?" Chuck peered closer.
"You've been crying, Sam! What happened?"

"Well, we just want different lives, that's all," Sammy
said as lightly as she could.

Chuck flipped the cup towel in the air. "Seems to me,"
he said with exaggerated indifference, "that the Air Force
wouldn't be so bad if you really loved your guy."

"It seems to me that Los Ladinos shouldn't be so bad for

a man who loved me," Sammy, retorted. "When did you take up marriage counseling?"

"Just now quit it," Chuck growled. He draped the towel over her arm. "Since you're here, I'll finish packing. Set your alarm for five o'clock. We've got to leave early so you can be back here at a decent hour."

Sammy covered her mouth with her hand. She'd forgotten! She was to take Chuck to College Station in the morning. How could she drive around the campus where she and Whit had walked and had fun when she came up for dances or ball games?

"I—I can't take you now, Chuck! I just can't."

Puffing out his cheeks, Chuck collapsed them explosively. "Yeeks, Sam, don't pull a female on me! I've got tons of stuff and Whit says the bus takes forever. Say, want me to call him and see if he wants a ride?"

"Your ideas get better and better!"

"Well, gosh!" Chuck's brown eyes were plaintive. "You get mad at him and who suffers? Me! If you won't drive, I'll have to leave my tennis racquet and golf clubs and radio and record player and—"

Sammy shut her ears with her hands. "All right! I'll bound up at five and off we go."

Chuck was going to be at A & M for four years. She'd be there several times a year on his account, and couldn't permit the luxury of avoiding the place she remembered in terms of Whit: Whit marching with his squadron past the reviewing stand, Whit at dances in the white dress uniform of A & M's honor military society, the Ross Volunteers, Whit playing basketball. But mostly Whit looking down at her with his sweet smile.

She straightened, wiping dishes briskly as she felt her twin's speculative eye on her. "Why don't you enroll at some college, Sam? Texas University or Baylor or maybe Rice? There's still time, and we could have fun getting each other dates and yelling for different schools."

Their parents' savings and insurance were enough to give both twins a college education and a little to start their adult lives. Sammy had never planned on more school, though. She didn't want to leave Los Ladinos, and she'd been so sure that Whit wanted to marry her that any other future had never crossed her mind.

She considered the prospect now without enthusiasm.

Beyond Whit and Los Ladinos, she had no ambition. She loved ranch life, Spanish customs, and children, but she couldn't think of anything she wanted to do that would require college.

Also, Whit's change of feeling made her cling even more tightly to Los Ladinos and the timeless, charmed life of it, to Martín and Chispa and Uncle Voss, to the songs of Tomás and the *vaqueros* as they rode out each morning.

"There's no reason for me to go to school," she told her twin.

Chuck tousled back his short red hair. "Golly, Sam, what will you do? I hate to go off and leave you all un-anchored!"

"Don't worry," she advised him. "I'll take the kids to school and back, run the house, ride, and——" A sudden flaring idea tingled through her. "And I'll get that coyote dun corraled and broken! That's what!" She explained about the wild horse the men had sighted out in the little hills.

"You're nuts," said Chuck, shaking his head. "Absolutely nuts! Breaking a range-wild horse is work for a top *vaquero*, with spurs and iron in his wrists. Don't try it, Sam."

"I can ride as well as you," she shot back. "Remember that bay mare who threw you? I trained her, didn't I? What's more——"

"Uncle Voss'll put a damper on that notion fast," Chuck warned. "You just want to break the horse because you couldn't get a bit in old Whit's mouth. Better wise up to yourself, kid!"

"Why——" began Sammy angrily when Uncle Voss filled the door.

"Quit scrapping, twins, and come in here," he drawled. "I've got something for Chuck."

Vengefully muttering, "I hope it's a swift kick!" Sammy preceded her brother into the living room. Her grumbling stopped in a swallow, though, as she blinked and stared at the highly polished riding boots.

Custom-made for her father when he'd been a senior at A & M, these boots, along with his decorations and sword, were the family pride. Only Corps seniors got to wear the boots with their smartly tailored dress uniforms, though of course all members of the Corps of Cadets wore uniforms throughout the school year.

Mingled with the pain of missing her father came another stabbing hurt. Whit would have boots this year. But she wouldn't be the girl he'd ask up for dances and ball games. Strange how little his life would change compared to hers. Sammy gazed at the boots through a haze of resentful, lonely tears.

How simple, how beautifully uncomplicated it was to be a man! A man didn't have to depend so much on love or people. He just picked a career and his girl went along with it or gave him up, and either way, he had something vital left, for his work could mean all that love and marriage went to women.

Who, for instance, was going to wear the heirloom boots in the Forrester family? Chuck, naturally! And it did not cheer Sammy to think that, after all, she could never have walked around in the things.

Chuck picked up the boots reverently, cradled them against his cheek, and watching him, the resentment left Sammy and she ached with pride in her brother and father. It was something, anyway, to glory in your men.

"These have always been seven-league boots to me," Chuck murmured. "I wonder if I'll ever fit them—not my big feet, you know, but *me?*"

Uncle Voss smiled. "You've got three years to reach the size of the cadet who wore them. Take 'em along and keep them in your locker or chest. There may come a time when it'll help you to take them out and handle them." He laughed, shaking his head. "The Corps doesn't whip and haze fish the way they did when your dad and I were in school, but I imagine that freshman year is still pretty rugged."

Sammy blinked and turned away. Aggravating as Chuck could be, she was going to miss him a lot. They'd never been separated for more than a week.

"You be sure to saddle-soap the boots often," she directed gruffly. "I'll put a tin of soap in your luggage so you won't forget."

She had to get out before she cried like a baby. Besides, it was a man's moment, a dead man's, whose brother and son were now honoring him, so Sammy went back through the kitchen to the supply room, got the saddle soap, and took it to Chuck's room.

A quick look showed he'd forgotten his socks, handkerchiefs, and dress shirts. Gratefully, she pitched into the task of getting his luggage ready. She tried not to think of the other Aggie, ten miles away, who was packing his boots. Without any help from her, without wanting any.

Uncle Voss was going to take the ranch children to school in the pickup so that Sammy could drive Chuck to College Station in the station wagon. After early breakfast the ranch people came to tell Chuck good-by.

Old Martín, his age-scarred face sad, Jorge, Comanche-blooded Vicente, young Tomás, and his older brothers—they all gravely shook hands, while their women stood in the doors of their cottages down by the unused bunkhouse, and waved. Lupe came to Chuck last. Slipping a parcel into his hands, she pulled his face down and kissed him, patted his cheeks.

"Go with God, my Chuck. You will be a pretty young officer and all the girls will love you. But do not forget your people and Los Ladinos."

He bent and hugged her. "Gosh, Lupe, I'm not going to the North Pole or anything! I'll be home for Thanksgiving and Christmas." He sniffed the package she'd given him. "Mmmm! That pecan candy of yours! Any time you think I need reminding of home, just send me a box of this."

Sliding under the wheel, he raised his hand to the little crowd. "So long, Uncle Voss. *Vaya con Dios*, Martín. *Adiós*, Lupe, *adiós, amigos!*" They drove off, and as they stopped at the iron gate, Chuck looked sheepishly at Sammy.

"I want to go to A & M, but I hate to leave the ranch. Crazy!"

"No." She gave his ear an affectionate tug. "You're just growing up."

"How can you tell?" he snorted. "Seeing as how you've got no experience." After the gate was closed and they were on the highway, Chuck seemed as eager to talk as she. This parting was proving harder than either had expected.

The country didn't change much until they headed east out of San Antonio. Trees began to clothe the country and hilled vistas faded away into the distance. The warm breeze had a touch of autumn in it, or perhaps it seemed so to

Sammy because she felt lonesome. About noon, clipping down Highway Number 6 she saw the gray pile of the administration building, the United States and Texas flags, and the smokestacks.

Last time she'd been here had been the Junior Prom. She'd had such a wonderful time all that day and evening, and Whit had refused to let his friends cut in, saying he didn't have enough dances even though his name was beside every single one . . . Chuck's voice snatched her back to reality.

"I'll pay my fees and get assigned to a squadron right now so we can unload my stuff. Then you'd better have a last big dinner on me before you start back."

Sammy grinned. "So long as I don't have to slip the money under the table to you, sir."

She waited in the station wagon, ignoring the inquiring looks of the cadet officers and freshmen who strolled by. Corps officers had to report early to get their organizations set up, while freshmen came a week ahead of classes for orientation. She realized, with a disgusted jump, whom she was watching for.

Whit.

There was stupidity for you. Such behavior was foolish, useless, not to be allowed.

She rummaged in the glove compartment for something to read, came up with a battered old road map. She had the mileage between every city in Texas figured out before Chuck finally reappeared.

"Whew!" he sighed, rubbing his brow. "It sho' starts off rugged! But I have a place to lay my head. If we can just find it!"

After some driving they found the barracks and parked as nearby as possible. Chuck got out the first installment of his gear and Sammy carried his portable radio. As they came up the walk, two cadet officers stepped out of Chuck's barracks. One was thin and blond with a pleasant smile. The other was stocky and powerful-looking, with a black burr and hazel eyes. He barred Chuck's way, cocking his head to one side.

"You billeted here, sonny?"

Chuck's neck stiffened. "Except for 'sonny,' you've got it right. My name's Chuck Forrester." The officer made a mock bow.

"Charmed." Straightening, he rapped out his words. "I'm your first sergeant, Forrester. You'd better like whatever I call you. Now stand at attention!"

Glaring, Chuck held to his suitcases. Before the first sergeant could take the matter further, the blond boy eased over.

"Why don't you unload your baggage, Forrester, and after chow you can go and get your uniforms?" He turned to the other cadet. "Mr. Ragan, I'll take over while you eat."

The sergeant didn't like it, but the three stainless steel buttons on the other officer's shirt showed that he was a captain, probably the squadron commander. Ragan saluted and left. Chuck proceeded ahead, leaving Sammy stranded with the cadet.

"I'll carry that radio," he said, taking it. "You're Forrester's *sister,* I hope."

Sammy laughed. "His twin. Thanks for rescuing him. I'm afraid Chuck may have a few hard lessons to learn."

"All fish do. But you might put a bug in his ear about tangling with Ragan. It won't get him anything but trouble. Sit here in the guard room, Miss Forrester, and I'll give your brother a hand. I'm Don Stuart."

His grip was strong and friendly. "Hello, Don," Sammy said and took a chair.

By the time Chuck was unloaded, the sergeant was back, so Don Stuart joined the twins at lunch in the Memorial Student Center. The long, handsome stone building dedicated to Aggies who had died in war, had huge plate-glass windows and giant planters ornamenting the outside. A plaque near the entrance listed the many Aggie dead. Above the names was embossed: GREATER LOVE HATH NO MAN THAN THIS, THAT A MAN LAY DOWN HIS LIFE FOR HIS FRIENDS. In honor of these soldiers no man wore a hat inside the building.

Sammy preceded her two companions through the cafeteria line. As they sat down in a booth, she saw Whit at a back table with two other seniors. He saw her at the same moment and raised his hand.

"Hi, Sammy."

For a plunging second their eyes held. Forcing a smile, Sammy waved back, turned to find Don studying her with curious gray eyes. "You know Whit Granger? He was top cadet of his summer camp and I hear he's a wing commander in the Corps this year."

"We come from the same cactus fields down near Zapata," Sammy said, trying for a note of gay insouciance. If Whit was watching her, she wanted him to think she was having a fine time.

"Why, you're not far from my home town, San Antonio," Don said. "Do you ever go there?"

"That's where I shop, mostly," Sammy answered. She went on talking, assuming a sparkle she didn't feel, keeping her gaze from Whit with great effort. Not to be his date this year, not even to get letters . . . She didn't realize that he was standing by the booth until he spoke:

"Have a good drive up?"

She nodded. Chuck grinned. "It was the registration that was rugged!" Don and Whit both laughed.

"You haven't seen anything yet, son," Whit warned. "Well, be careful driving home, Sam. See you around."

Where? As he turned and left, Sammy clenched her hands. All right, she'd do as he said! Tonight she'd be back at Los Ladinos behind the sun-warmed walls where Lupe lighted candles by San Isidro and Martín mounted in the name of God. She'd stay there and hear Tomás sing through the fall and winter; see if this pain and sense of loss and loving Whit would fade.

CHAPTER THREE

When she struck the cactus country again, leaving the trees, dusk was coming on. The loneliness of the wasteland swooped down on her, doubled by her good-by to Chuck and the last glimpse of Whit. Tomás' song beat a refrain in her ears:

"Because, anyway, in the world there are other lovers.
 As I loved you, so can I forget you."

She told herself that the smart of her eyes was caused by wind and dust. Going the speed limit, eating up the miles back to Los Ladinos, Sammy wondered how she would ever get through the long months till the Ring Dance. And suppose nothing was changed then? What if she and Whit still loved each other but were adamant about their plans?

I don't worry about that now, she vowed. Maybe I can get Uncle Voss interested in breeding a mustang line—especially if I can catch and tame that coyote dun. *And come up for dances with Don Stuart?* He had hinted he might ask her. Right now she couldn't bear thinking about dates with anyone but Whit, but later on . . . He'd said they had to be sure, hadn't he?

Her mind ticked restlessly as she drove. It was dark and the miles seemed longer. Not too far from the turn-off to the ranch, she saw a red light.

Border Patrol? They sometimes spot-checked cars. Pulling over to stop, Sammy saw in the dim light that the car was plain and the man coming toward her with his red-filter flashlight wore ordinary khakis, not a uniform.

It was too late now to roll up the windows, lock the doors. Sammy kept her foot on the accelerator for a fast start if it seemed advisable.

"Señorita!" The man was big and easy-moving like the wild cats still found in the brush country, and in the glare from the headlights his eyes burned green. Meet an *onza* . . . With a prickling of her scalp Sammy remembered Lupe's stories. *"Señorita,"* he went on, a note of perplexity in his deep, slow voice, *"mi camisa está perdida* and—and —darn it all, do you speak any English? *Habla inglés?"*

If this was an *onza,* he spoke awful Spanish. Sammy fought back a chuckle. He had taken her for a Latin and powerfully mangled the language. Instead of meaning that he had lost his shirt, *camisa,* he must mean he'd lost his road, *camino.*

"I speak English a little, *Señor,"* she replied wickedly. "You haven't lost your shirt at all; it's on your back. What *camino* are you hunting?"

"Doggone it!" A grin sloped down one corner of his mouth and he pushed his hand through his short sandy hair. "I sure picked the wrong languages tonight all around. The last two trucks I stopped didn't understand any English. They must have thought I was crazy when I kept telling them I'd lost my shirt." He put back his head and laughed, enjoying his own mistake though it must have caused him an aggravating wait. Sammy found herself drawn to him, and curious.

"Most folks around here speak at least some English, anyway the men do. You just had unusual luck tonight. What road do you want?"

"I'm looking for the road that leads to the eastern curve of Tigre Creek. I've been down it once, but that was in daylight. Now I can't find it to save my neck."

Sammy thought a minute, snapped her fingers. "Sure, I ride that way sometimes! It turns off close to our north boundary. It's pretty well hidden by brush. Follow me and I'll spot it for you."

"Thanks," he said with heartfelt relief. "That's mighty nice of you."

"De nada, Señor," laughed Sammy. From the start of her life here, she'd loved the language and now spoke it well. If this stranger intended to prowl the brush, he'd better learn Spanish or get an interpreter.

What was he doing on Tigre Creek? As he got in his sleek little sports car, he stuck on a hat and Sammy saw that it was the kind of helmet worn by oil workers.

About a mile down the road, she saw the great guarded *retama* that marked the end of their northern range. Slowing, she guided the station wagon to pinpoint the entrance of the road. About ten yards north of the *retama,* hidden by a tangle of mesquite and sage, was a three-strand "Texas gate" or barbed-wire.

"There it is," Sammy called back to the stranger. "I don't know if you can get that car through the tangle, though."

"I've got a machete," he said, climbing out and crossing to her: "Failing that, I can always pick the bug up and carry it." He dropped his arms on the window, leaning down to look at her, and Sammy's nervousness rushed back. Involuntarily she drew away from the window.

"Hey!" he protested. "I only want to know who led me safely through the jungle. I'm Lee McAllen, from Forth Worth, though I don't spend much time there."

"I'm Sammy Forrester. I live with my uncle at Los Ladinos."

"Is that the old horse ranch right south of here?"

Sammy nodded.

"Then I'll probably see you soon," the tall man said as he straightened. "Good night, Sammy, and thanks." He strode over to his car and got out the long-bladed machete. Sammy put the station wagon in gear and was home in twenty minutes.

The stranger already seemed like a thing she'd dreamed up, yet she felt better than she had before he stepped out of the dark.

If he was an *onza,* she thought, smiling, he was a nice one. His eyes knew a lot about people and life. He had frightened her a little, but he had acted and talked like a kind person. Uncle Voss came out on the veranda, eager to hear about Chuck's arrival at school, and Sammy put Lee McAllen out of her mind, at least for a while.

The eight youngsters who went to school, ranging in age from six to eleven, were waiting by the station wagon when Sammy hurried out next morning. Besides Tomás, there were his brother, Jorge's three children, eight-year-old Soledad and the twins, Rudi and Juana, who were just starting first grade. Also six was Chuey Montes, Vicente's only child. The other three children were from the neighboring Tres Hermanos ranch, Ana and Javier Cruz and Miguel Luna. Javier was taking the first grade again and Miguel and Ana were second-graders.

Counting noses, Sammy smiled a greeting to the children and watched them clamor in. How wrong some people were who thought Latins all looked alike!

As she halted at the iron gate and Tomá jumped out to open it, she asked her passengers, "How do you like school this year?"

Dead silence.

Puzzled, Sammy drove through the gate and waited for Tomás to hop in before she tried again. Tomás spoke English very well, but the younger children knew varying amounts and the first-graders hardly any. That was why Javier Cruz had failed last year. So, thinking perhaps she hadn't been understood, Sammy spoke in Spanish.

"Les gustan a ustedes sus maestras?" Are pleasing to you your teachers?

Tomás, Soledad, Ana, and Miguel nodded with more or less sincerity, but the first-graders stared glumly at the floor, with expressions ranging from Javier's despair to Rudi's contempt.

Soledad primmed her new gingham skirt and spoke with

the superiority of a third-grader with a new permanent and gold earbobs.

"Their teacher doesn't have *any* Spanish. They can't understand what she says."

"Good grief! That's a mess all way around." Sammy glanced at Soledad. "Does your teacher speak Spanish?"

"No, but my first and second-grade teachers did whenever we couldn't understand what they meant in English. Now," Soledad added proudly, "I know much English."

"Don't you speak it at home?" Sammy knew that Jorge both read and wrote English, and she had supposed it was used in his house.

With a stare of shock Soledad shook her head. "Oh no, Señorita Sam! Mama is from Saltillo and never even heard English till Papa brought her here. I wouldn't be correct to speak a language she doesn't know, *verdad?*"

"I suppose so," was all Sammy could say.

She had never thought about it, but she could see why many women in rural areas usually at home all day and meeting only other Latins, never learned English. Even in bilingual homes, Spanish was used unless "Anglos" were present. There were pre-primer classes designed to teach a little basic English to Spanish-speaking children, but these evidently couldn't bridge the gap between a non-Spanish speaking teacher and a Latin group.

This was bound to be a tragic handicap in school where one misunderstood word could make a big difference in what was asked and what was done. Rudi's lip quivered.

"The *maestra* is very beautiful," she said in Spanish. "But I do not know what she wants me to do. She thinks I am a burro—*muy tonto!*"

Javier nodded, pointing to his red shirt front.

"Well!" said Sammy without thinking beyond the sad little faces, "we'll fix this!" And then she tried to think how.

She liked the children and, anyway, as the *patrón's* niece she was responsible for the well-being of the Los Ladinos people. "I'll talk to your teacher," she promised. "Don't worry, *chicos!* I'm sure she and I can work something out."

Chuey hugged Sammy so hard that she almost drove into the ditch. Sammy yipped warningly before the others could join in.

"Hold off, kids! The wagon can't drive itself. Let's sing

something." This was always good strategy to fill in the forty-minute drive. "How about the coyote song?"

"Ride through the prickly pear, pass the *mogote*.
Go tell to your mother that you saw the coyote . . ."

Singing along, Sammy listened especially for Tomás' clear voice. This was Uncle Voss' favorite ballad—or had been till Loney began eating watermelons. As they switched to other songs, Sammy muted her singing in order to hear the children better. All the time she worked at the English problem.

Talking to the teacher was fine, but in itself it wouldn't solve things. Wasn't there some way to help the children speed up their comprehension of English? *Now*, before they got discouraged or fell hopelessly behind? Parking in front of the long stucco building, Sammy followed the first-graders down the arched porch to their room, smiling and waving to other children she knew. Also growing more nervous by the minute.

How was the teacher going to like it, a total outsider barging in and probing at what was bound to be a sore spot? Quaking inwardly, Sammy stepped through the door.

Someone had been at work! Although the room was a drab, discouraged yellow, with unpainted wooden floors, it fairly glowed with color. Mother Goose people and circus animals marched around the wall top, ivy plants in gay bowls livened window ledges, and on top of the piano was a beautiful crystal vase filled with red roses. A flannel board held red, blue, and yellow umbrellas and ducks.

Sun slanted past the palms outside the windows and pointed a shaft of gold toward the girl who stood by a record player, sorting albums. Their bright jackets bore pictures of cowboys, mermaids, ballerinas. Sammy suspected that the teacher had paid for them out of her own pocket.

Convoyed by the children, Sammy walked toward the other girl, who looked up with a questioning smile.

Nails and lips tinted a gay spice red, with a fair complexion that set off russet hair and eyes, she wore a smoothly fitted beige skirt and blouse. Sammy forgot her prepared speech and glowed with honest admiration.

"If teaching can help a girl to look like you, I'd better take it up," she laughed. "I'm Sammy Forrester from Los Ladinos. The kids told me about their *lindísima* teacher. They were right!"

"*Lindísima?*"

"The perfect absolute of 'beautiful.' The which there's no more than." Sammy gave Rudi and the others a pat, sending them off.

The teacher smiled, and Sammy realized that there couldn't be over five years' difference in their ages. "Thanks, Miss Forrester. I'm Fran Murdoch. . . . Is there something you want to discuss?" The last words came out a bit stiffly. It occurred to Sammy that the other girl was on the defensive and perhaps not much more used to such conversations than she, Sammy, was.

Somehow that made it easier to talk, and smile while doing it. "I'm not trying to interfere, Miss Murdoch, but some of your children know so little English that they're having trouble. I wonder if there's some way they can be helped."

"I don't speak Spanish," said the older girl somewhat abruptly. "Even if I did, I'm running a first grade, not a language course."

"Of course. But some of the students will fail if things go on as they are."

Fran sat down. Tiredly, she pushed at her softly waving hair. "I'm afraid you're right. I was told that I wouldn't have been hired here except for an awful shortage because I'm not bilingual, so I had some hint of the problem. But I didn't think it would be as bad as it is. I try to act things out and use pictures and songs and games to stimulate a natural growth of the language, but that takes time! Besides, they won't tell me when they don't understand things. They just let me go on. It's when I give tests and collect homework that I find out I wasn't understood at all!" She blew upward at a wispy curl and her look at Sammy was somewhere between appeal and challenge. "You know the kids, and I gather you're bilingual. Do you have any ideas?"

"Well——" Sammy felt foolish to mention teaching to anyone who had gone to college and earned a degree, but it was the only suggestion she could think of. "Maybe I could have sort of a class at our ranch in the evening. Sing songs, handle objects, and name them. That sort of thing."

She ended on an apologetic note, sure that Fran would feel encroached upon, but the older girl was instantly on her feet, relief vibrating in her tone.

"Would you really do that? Anything would be a help! I—I . . . Last night I went home and cried, even thought about resigning and all kinds of desperate deeds. I do intend to take Spanish lessons, but I think my youngsters can learn English faster than I can learn Spanish. I've heard it advocated to teach foreign languages to eight-year-olds, before they lose their powers of imitation. Wish I'd learned then!"

At the ringing of the first bell Sammy jumped up. "Then I'll see what I can work out. I'll be happy to work with other children besides those that ride with me. Shall we have a session tonight?"

"The sooner the better," Fran said emphatically. "I'll try to get permission from the parents of the other non-English speaking youngsters during the noon hour. Why don't I bring out a carload and sit in on the lessons too?"

"Fine, if you won't expect too much. I may talk Doodle-bug—one of our ranch hands—into coming after the kids tonight since I'll be pretty rushed. But you can follow him out to the ranch. Be seeing you around four!"

With a wave to the children, Sammy ran out. As she got into the wagon, she was breathless, and not just from hurrying.

She had just wanted to help the ranch children and a few of the neighboring ones. Now it seemed that she might wind up with half the first grade—plus a real honest-to-goodness teacher who might find plenty to criticize in whatever she could devise in the way of teaching methods.

Sammy squared her shoulders. What did the children need to know? English. Basic, necessary English.

She knew that, didn't she? She also knew their language and something about how they reacted. If she wanted to give them what she could, and they wanted to receive, the means would develop out of their mutual interest and contact. Whoa! She stepped on the brake and pulled in by the general store that handled school supplies.

While she was in town, she'd better get a few things to start class with. The old bunkhouse, no longer in use since all the *vaqueros* were married, could be cleaned out and used for a school. Maybe some of the men could fix chairs or benches. And she could hang up a blackboard that she and Chuck had used as a bulletin board, and find some pictures and . . .

Laden with chalk, pencils, crayons, paper, plastic animals, and people, Sammy dropped her loot on the kitchen table.

"Escuela, escuela!" she sang to Lupe's startled glance. "I'm going to have English school. Won't it be fun?" She gave a long, trilling whistle and danced the resisting Lupe a few measures.

"You are loco, I think," Lupe groaned, pinning up a braid that had come loose. "You already speak the English. Why should you go to school?"

"Oh, it isn't for me, Lupe! It's for Rudi and Juana and Chuey and Javier Cruz and a lot of others! To help them speak English faster so school won't be so hard."

Lupe frowned and motioned to a plate in the warming oven. "I don't know about that, Sammy-*Mula,* but you sit down and eat right now. Your uncle has already gone back to work."

It was no good, ever, to argue with Guadalupe. Sammy ate, pouring out her plans between bites, with the result that Lupe warmed to the project and promised cookies and lemonade to get things off to a festive start. Doodlebug came in late too, and volunteered his help. He loved the children, perhaps because they never tired of his oil-field stories and would sit spellbound for hours, listening to him.

While Doodlebug nailed up the blackboard and constructed benches with plank backs, Sammy swept, mopped, and dusted. The open windows and door gradually banished the musty smell, though it was pitilessly hot to be working hard.

Still, this was better, oh much better, than crying over Whit. It felt good to be useful and busy. Uncle Voss was fond of saying a person could think of only one thing at a time. Sammy decided she'd take that for her motto. She'd work so hard and think so hard about other things that she wouldn't have strength or time to mourn. When the essential cleaning was done, she stood in the center of the room and surveyed her possibilities—and limitations.

Well, was her first defensive, disappointed reaction,

they're supposed to learn, not admire the surroundings. Her unsatisfied eye continued to rove, however, and she soon had a few inspirations.

Bright curtains would almost change the room. A coat of whitewash on the wall would cover up the marks and dirt. Didn't she still have that big serape that could cover up the worst splinters and protect little hands and knees and seats? Some place she had piles of Southwestern pictures: horses, missions, roundups, Indians.

Selecting and rejecting ideas, her mind tumbled swiftly. Japanese lanterns. One of the bunks turned into a couch with serapes and a bolster. That old rocking chair from the guest bedroom. A first-aid kit, some of the games she and Chuck had played . . .

Back and forth between the bunkhouse and *casa grande* Sammy and Doodlebug went. Curtain and whitewash would have to wait. But by three o'clock the benches were grouped on the ombre serape, Japanese lanterns drew attention from the stained ceiling, and a Japanese screen hid the unused bunkhouse furniture while adding an exotic splash of color. Doodlebug had nailed a paper-cup dispenser by the door and on the table beneath them was the huge insulated jug of lemonade and ice Lupe had made.

Sammy had only had time to put up one picture. It was a painting from her own room that Uncle Voss had given her, a group of mustangs racing across the brushland, herded by a magnificent black stallion. You could almost hear and feel the stinging rush of sun and wind, smell the salt cedar, and hear the wild hoofs.

Back in the house, Sammy showered and dressed, sighing with pleasure at the feel of being clean again as she slipped into fresh cotton clothes. Physical preparation had taken the whole day. Now, as she brushed her hair and put on lipstick, she reasoned that the best way to teach a word was to associate it with the proper object or action and then drill, drill, drill. But after a day in school, the children would have to find the work interesting, and fun.

For that night's session Sammy unearthed a candlestick, an old clock, and some paper dolls. She took these over to the bunkhouse and was tacking the dolls to the blackboard rim when the grinding of a car in the drive sent her to the door.

Goodness, Doodlebug had just left a few minutes ago to

drive after the children. Fran must have dismissed class early to be here this fast. Sammy looked out and blinked in amazement.

No carload of children were wriggling out of the car—in fact, they couldn't have for it was a little black sports car. The person coming up the path was a big man with broad shoulders, an oil man's hat, and he was carrying—yes, what looked like a florist's box though it was eighty miles to the nearest one.

CHAPTER FOUR

"The lady at the house said you were down here," Lee McAllen smiled, his green eyes so intently on her that Sammy flushed. "I've been wanting to thank you for your help last night."

"Oh, that's not necessary," she disclaimed.

"It's my pleasure."

Sammy was acutely conscious of his height and slow, smooth strength as he came up the plank steps and looked down at her. He put the long white box into her hands. "You'd better open this inside. It's hot enough here to fry roses on exposure."

Within the building, Lee cut the string for her and then glanced around the room in surprise. "Say, what is this?"

"Three guesses," countered Sammy, undoing the green waxed paper.

"I don't know. Serapes, lanterns, Japanese screens———" His sunburned brows yanked together. A note of horror took the drawl out of his voice. "Say, this isn't a nursery, is it? You—you don't have any kids?"

"What's wrong with children?" Sammy asked, unable to resist a chance to tease. "Don't you like them?"

"Sure, but———" Before she could guess his intention, he turned her left hand around, straightened the fingers with his long tanned ones. "No ring!"

He sounded so relieved that Sammy couldn't resent it, or the humorous mockery of his tone as he put her hand back on the box. "A little thought would have told me you're too young to have populated all those benches. But what is the place?"

"It's sort of an English school. I just got the idea today, so it's not fixed up too well——" She broke off in delight as the last green paper fell away and she held up the flowers.

Long-stemmed crimson roses, gallant and gay, ranging from buds to full blooms. Sammy's experience with flowers had been limited to Whit's corsages for several A & M dances. She couldn't breathe for a second. Bringing them close to her face, she luxuriated in their fragrance, the velvety touch of the petals on her lips and cheek.

"They're lovely," she sighed. "But, really, you shouldn't have——"

"Had the fun of watching you enjoy them!"

Something in his gaze, questioning behind the warm amusement, made Sammy turn and hunt up a jar to put the roses in.

"I'll move them to a vase in the house later," she said, filling the jar with water from the faucet that had once sloshed full the *vaqueros'* washbowls. "My children should get here any minute so I can't honor these properly right now."

"You are. You're touching them."

At a boy her own age, Sammy would have laughed. There was no laughing at Lee McAllen and for a second, she was almost afraid. You, *onza*, you with your lazy smile and green eyes ∙ . . .

"I'm teaching some of the Latin children English," she said, desperately grasping at ordinary conversation.

He let her escape, though the quirk of his mouth showed that he saw through her effort. "I could use that class, in reverse. May I audit this session?"

"No!" she panicked. "Not tonight," she added when he looked hurt. "I've never done anything like this. I need time. If you'd like to drop by in a week or two, when I sort of know what I'm doing, I'd be glad to have you."

"Fine." He stood in the doorway a minute. "I'll have to talk to your uncle later anyway. Your housekeeper said he was gone." Before Sammy could ask why he needed to see Uncle Voss, Lee nodded and went down the steps.

Bemused, Sammy put the roses on the table she planned to use as a desk. They were extravagant, and though they buoyed up her spirits, they troubled her too. Surely he

could have found a simpler way to say thanks. And yet—
bending down, breathing in their sweet smell and laughed
—she was happy he had brought them.

Cars in the drive, slamming doors, and children's voices
roused her. Running to the door, she called her thanks to
Doodlebug and started counting the bobbing heads sur-
rounding her.

Two—four—eight—twelve!

"You'll have more tomorrow," Fran informed her,
waving from the outskirts. "I couldn't contact all the parents today. Are you ready?"

"Come in," gulped Sammy. "We'll both find out!"

The children sighted the roses and zeroed in with cries
of, *"Lindísima!"* Sammy took the opportunity to explain
in English, with strategic gestures, that the roses were red,
their leaves were green, and they sat on the table in a jar.

Then, in Spanish, she welcomed the youngsters, asked
the names of the few she didn't recognize, and explained
that she would do things, naming the action in English
which they would repeat.

Since they were hot and thirsty after their ride, she
began the lesson by filling a paper cup with lemonade.

"I fill the cup. I drink." Motioning to Juana who sat first
on the bench, Sammy spoke distinctly: "Juana, come. Tell
me. I fill the cup. I drink."

Juana triumphantly worked the spigot, repeated the
words, and drank. She went back to her seat like the general of a conquering army. When all the children had served
themselves, and Fran had a cup, Sammy led the way by the
wastebasket.

"I throw the cup in the wastebasket." This was echoed
by twelve actions, twelve voices.

Back at their places, the children followed Sammy
through a series of action phrases.

"I sit down. I stand up. I walk. I jump. I tie my shoe."
After they repeated these several times, Sammy used a
mixture of English and Spanish to tell the children about
the paper-doll family and then asked questions, illustrated
with motions, which could be answered with yes, no, or a
single word.

"Qué color tiene los ojos de el bebé?" Sammy asked.
"What color are the eyes of the baby? Are they black?
Blue? Pink? Yes, Rudi, they are *café*—brown. What color

is his toy bear? *Azul? Verde?* Oh, that's right, Chuey. It is *amarillo.* Yellow."

From the family, they moved to the candlestick. Placing it in the middle of the floor, Sammy brought Fran over and admonished her:

> "*Maestra,* be nimble, *maestra,* be quick!
> *Maestra,* jump over the candlestick!"

On "jump," Fran acted. The children clapped and squealed. Their pretty new teacher was playing with them! Javier jumped next, and the children joined in the chant:

> "Javier, be nimble, Javier, be quick!
> Javier, jump over the candlestick!"

After a few repetitions of the whole rhyme, Sammy led the whole group in leaping over the stick and saying, "I jump!" And when it came Fran's turn, Sammy taught her to say, *"Yo brinco!"*

There was just time for "One-two, buckle my shoe" before five o'clock and time to take the children home. The Tres Hermanos and Los Ladinos dwellers scattered. Sammy helped Fran corral the seven who lived back toward town.

"It was marvelous!" Fran said. "I can learn so much about the kids from watching this, and it should speed up my Spanish. That room showed a lot of work. Are you exhausted?"

"I loved it all," Sammy laughed. "I'm sure you saw some ways I could improve the class though. Could you come back for dinner and tell me?"

"If I get any good ideas, I'll let you know. Right now I'm trying to figure out how to persuade Diego Ruiz to let his little boy take your lessons. Mr. Ruiz almost took my head off when I asked." She grimaced. *"He* speaks English."

A picture of Diego watching his drowned village at sundown shot before Sammy's eyes. She said, "He's had a pretty rough time. His old home, Zapata, was flooded when Falcón was built, and he's mad at changes."

"Possibly so. But Carlos has to learn English some time, so why does his father make it hard?" Fran pushed her hair back, put the car in gear. "Wish I could accept that dinner invitation, but I've got piles of work. Maybe Friday?" She bit her lip. "Oops, sorry. That'll be date night for you."

Sammy fought down a stab of bitterness. "Not exactly. We'll expect you then around seven. Will you come to class tomorrow?"

"Wouldn't miss it for the world," Fran vowed. She drove off and Sammy stood in the road waving good-by to various small brown arms protruding from the windows.

They liked it and they learned. Smiling at memories, planning new activities, Sammy went to the school and tidied up. She would have real news to write Chuck tonight! She hoped his new experiences were off to as interesting a start. If he could just keep out of trouble with that first sergeant! Chuck was pretty much a mustang himself, hard to handle and quick to rebel. Uncle Voss had used a light rein on the twins and the tough Corps discipline was bound to rub Chuck the wrong way. Those boots of Dad's had better exert a powerfully inspiring, calming influence.

Sammy picked up the roses and carried them to the house. As she filled a crystal vase for them, Lupe surveyed the flowers with mingled delight and misgiving.

"Where did you get these, Sammy-*Mula*? That stranger-man with green eyes? Who is he? Where did you meet him? Is he of good family?"

"He lost his way to Tigre Creek and I showed him the turnoff," Sammy said, seeing no use to add that it had been after dark. "He was grateful, I suppose, and brought the flowers. His name is Lee McAllen and he's from Fort Worth. His parents must be nice because he is."

"He also asked for the *patrón*. Why?"

Sniffing a rose, Sammy raised an imploring hand. "I don't know, Lupe. Why didn't you ask him?"

"Maybe next time I will. Only next time I hope the *patrón* will be here to determine whether this man should see you. Gifts from the wrong people are a reproach, not an honor."

Lupe could moralize for hours if she got started. Sammy hugged her, took the prettiest rose, and pinned it at a flirtatious angle behind Lupe's ear.

"Mr. McAllen must be all right or he wouldn't have wanted to see Uncle Voss. Your lemonade was so good!

The children loved it. Here, let me rub your neck where it gets tired and I'll tell you all about the school."

The days rushed by in busy hours of fixing curtains, whitewashing the walls, and finding ways to teach the basic English that would make school much easier for the children. Fran brought books from school and the teachers' collections, from which Sammy culled songs, games, rhymes.

She bought a family of small plastic dolls, let the children name, dress, and play with them, describing these pursuits in English. One corner of the room became a play-kitchen with toy dishes and utensils, and another corner became a play-store with empty cans and cartons stocking the box shelves.

"When some of them don't know *sink* can mean anything but going down in a marsh, this helps," Fran said, nodding at the make-believe sink, stove, and refrigerator that Doodlebug had crafted out of boxes and tin scraps. Her face clouded. "I wish Carlos Ruiz were coming. Of all those who can't speak English, he's the only one who isn't here."

"Maybe Diego will loosen up when he sees the boy is falling behind," Sammy hoped.

There were sixteen children coming now. Sammy and Fran brought them out after school, and since only eight had to be driven home, Fran managed that.

Fran was speaking some Spanish now, to the children's delight. It made them proud that their beautiful *maestra* was learning their language and they worked even harder to learn hers.

Busy as the days were, Sammy plunged gratefully into the work each new one brought. She thought of Whit— that she couldn't help, couldn't avoid. He had been part of her dreams too long. But the warm happiness in helping the children and being needed kept her from brooding, turning her thoughts and emotions in upon herself.

When she tried to look at the future, it was a solid wall. She fell back from it for now, she would work and live outside herself. She could get through each day, an hour at a time. Days made weeks, weeks grew into months. And after enough of them, she'd think of what to do.

Also, once she had the English school under control, she

meant to urge the *vaqueros* to watch for the coyote dun. He could be the start of a proud new line of Los Ladinos horses.

Friday noon they shared a letter from Chuck, Doodlebug and Uncle Voss grinning over his complaints about the way "fish" were treated:

> If I don't know the answer to something an upperclassman asks, I have to say—all in five seconds—"Sir, not being informed to the highest degree of accuracy, I hesitate to articulate for fear that I may deviate from the true course of rectitude. In short, sir, I am a very dumb fish and do not know, sir!"

Sammy groaned. "I bet that Sergeant Ragan is asking him a lot of those questions! They got off to a bad start."

"A few lumps won't hurt Chuck," Uncle Voss said. "Say, you made quite a hit with the squadron commander, Sam! He's been asking Chuck about you."

"He's nice," Sammy admitted. "I'm not eager to get mixed up with any more Aggies, though."

Uncle Voss raised his eyebrows until furrows grooved his leathery face. "That so? Then maybe you'd favor the oil man I'm having out tonight."

"Oil man?" gasped Doodlebug.

"Who?" demanded Sammy.

"You've met already—Lee McAllen. We're talking leases on our east range."

Clearing his throat, Doodlebug huffed with a dourness that couldn't conceal his anticipation. "He's probably like all the rest. A durn geologist with no blood in his veins." Still, he left before dessert to wander off with his forked peach twig.

"I'll have company too," Sammy told her uncle. "Fran Murdoch, the new first-grade teacher from El Sauz. She's a doll, reddish hair, pretty legs, sweet manners. You'll like her."

"I like all the ladies," twinkled Uncle Voss. "That's why I never married. Couldn't make up my mind."

"Didn't you ever ask *anyone*?"

His gray eyes touched her with an odd expression. "I

asked one girl . . . but she liked someone else better."

"Really?" asked Sammy, intrigued. She started to probe, but a tightening at the corners of her uncle's mouth told her that this was something he'd rather not discuss. Teasingly, she passed the subject over. "You're off after Loney too much to please a wife. If you caught that old coyote, you'd be sorry. You wouldn't have anything to hunt."

"I will be sorry if I catch her, but it's Loney or the melons." Uncle Voss sighed. "The older I get, the surer I am that life is a series of choices. Give up this to get that, keep this and let go of that—and whoever tries to hang onto everything winds up with nothing but skinned palms." He gave her an oblique glance. "Like that coyote dun Martín's been telling us about. We can have him tamed or have him free, but not both ways."

How could you know what I was planning? Sammy thought. It was her turn to draw tight her lips. "I want him tamed. You aren't sold on going all-out for horse-raising, Uncle Voss, but that's how I'd like to invest my share of Mother and Dad's estate." Excusing herself, she left the table.

Why did Uncle Voss have to make her feel guilty? It wasn't criminal to bring a wild horse in where he'd have grain and fine mares and shelter in the raw northers. Why, the dun could be the sire of a great line and Los Ladinos could regain its old glory.

As she went down the hall, Doodlebug stepped from one of the patio arches. "Miss Sam." His old hands trembled as they gripped the peach twig. "You reckon that oil friend of yours would hire me?"

"Why don't you ask him, Doodlebug? I'm sure he will if he has a place open."

"I kind of hate to. See, Miss Sam, when a man's old, it troubles a younger man's conscience, sort of, to turn him down. I don't want a job out of pity. But if he could use me, I'd sure be happy."

Did Doodlebug have absolutely no one? Had the dicky bird's song cut him off from all his family? He never received or sent mail. Except for oil stories, he never spoke of his past. Sammy didn't believe, at all, that money had been his driving urge. He had heard that weird cast-iron dicky bird and followed the shriek of the oil fields ever since.

"I'll ask Mr. McAllen," she promised. "But you be sure to eat with us tonight. You can talk about oil so well. Uncle Voss and I are ignorant about it and we'll need you." Doodlebug was smiling and stroking his peach twig when Sammy passed San Isidro and entered her room.

After English class Fran took the children home, saying she'd be back as soon as she showered and dressed. Sammy made a point of not dressing up for Lee's benefit, but she did wear her prettiest cut-work blouse and a border-printed skirt that fitted snug at the waist to flare a full circle at the hem. She brushed her hair till it reflected gleams of light and smoothed the uptilted line of her eyebrows till she looked positively Oriental.

She didn't want to get involved with Lee. Something warned her that he wasn't a man to treat casually and forget. But she didn't want Fran to totally eclipse her either.

Hurrying to the kitchen, Sammy helped Lupe with the rice and chicken and set the table. She picked a cinnamon cloth and napkins to see off the plain modern white china she had collected for her future—and possibly nonexistent —home. In a smoky-tinted beaker she placed three remaining roses.

"They're mighty tenacious to be so pretty," came an amused voice from the door. Sammy turned.

Lee McAllen stood there with a Stetson in his hand. With his light gray suit he wore a white shirt and black string tie that made his face darkly vivid.

"Come in," Sammy invited, laughing. "You look like a member of an honorary sheriff's posse or a rich cowman. Uncle Voss will be out in a minute. Would you like some iced tea to cool you off?"

"I'd appreciate it." He eyed her and the table so that she didn't know which he spoke about next. "Sure looks pretty. You folks have a nice place here."

"Thank you." Sammy glowed at his sincerity. She loved the ranch so much that a compliment about it was better than one to her. Suddenly remembering her promise to Doodlebug, she came right to the point. "Do you have any kind of work for—for an older man?"

"Depends on the older man," said Lee. "My father was shooting oil wells with nitroglycerin when he was seventy. What does your guy do?"

"He—well, he doodlebugs with a peach twig. He thinks it'll pull downward when he gets near oil."

"A doodlebug!" Lee chuckled, rubbing his jaw. "Well, what do you know? And with a peach twig yet. I figured they'd all switched over to hunting cobalt or uranium."

"You seem to think it's nonsense." Sammy's tone was cool. Doodlebug might be sort of odd, but he was good-hearted and by his very difference he added the dimension of dreams and will-o'-the-wisp to life.

It seemed to her that, like the buffalo and whooping crane, the Doodlebugs of this world ought to be preserved because they were unique and growing scarce. So she frowned at Lee McAllen.

"Don't glower," he said. "Just look at it my way. I went to work for Dad while I was still a kid. At college I took petroleum engineering and worked summers in the fields. All together, I've had nearly twelve years in oil. I've drilled dry holes and I've brought in gushers and there's no way to be right all the time about what you'll find down in the earth. If all the training and tests and scientific indications aren't reliable, what can you expect from a peach twig?"

Sammy bit her lip. For all his twenty-six years, he was a man who knew his business. What could she tell him about oil and people? "Doodlebug can witch for water too," she said. "He found the location of one of our wells. He says there's a power in him that can sense the water or oil, as a magnet draws iron."

"I don't know about that. But there's a power in some people and it doesn't have anything to do with oil. Look, I'll hire your Doodlebug on as a cook and handyman. I'm afraid roughnecking would be too hard on him. But I'll pick my own drilling sites."

"Then you won't ever hear the dicky bird," she warned.

"How'd you—oh, the old man told you! No, I don't suppose he'll sing to me. But Dad says he heard him. At Spindletop and Burkburnett when the wells came in with a roar like the earth exploding."

Delightedly Sammy clapped her hands. "Why, Doodlebug was at both places!"

"He claim to have peach-twigged 'em?"

"No." Sammy's pleasure died at the irony in Lee's voice. "I hope you aren't going to make the classic remark—that

if he can find oil, why isn't he rich? If you do, I'll—
I'll——"

A golden light leaped and flickered in Lee's eyes. A smile
tugged at his straight mouth. "Will you beat me up? Pound
me with your fists?"

"Oh!" choked Sammy in exasperation. "Be serious!"

"All right. I'll hire your friend, but I won't drill a well
because his twig points in that direction. Shake on that?"

"Why, sure!" laughed Sammy. She put out her hand.
Lee's, fitting over it, was so strong and warm that she
quickly ended the handshake. "Excuse me," she said, flus-
tered. "I'll go get your tea."

CHAPTER FIVE

Uncle Voss, because of Fran, had duded himself up in a tie
and a white shirt, but he talked Lee out of keeping on his
coat before they all settled comfortably at the table.

"The looks of teachers have certainly improved since I
used to trudge up for my daily switching," Uncle Voss told
Fran. "How about this English school, Miss Murdoch? It
is helping the kids?"

Fran sparkled with enthusiasm. "You can't imagine, Mr.
Forrester! In just one week it's made a big change. The
children try to use English even at recess, and they don't
mind telling me now when they don't understand what I
mean. It helps *la maestra* too! Before long I'll know what
the little tykes are saying when they look my way and
giggle."

Pouring tea and passing the lemon, Sammy asked, "Have
you talked to Diego Ruiz again?"

"You might call it that." Fran knit her brows. "I stopped
by, intending to talk to Mrs. Ruiz this time, but she doesn't
know any English. So Mr. Ruiz pinned my ears back again.
He said that his children may have to go to school but they
don't have to study English after hours and I couldn't make
them. Which is true." She stared at her slim fingers. "He
seems to have a grudge against me."

"It's time he woke up," Sammy said indignantly.

Uncle Voss shook his head. "Getting cooperation from

Diego is mighty hard these days. He had to move from Zapata and he sees everything in terms of being pushed around."

"Can't he see he's hurting Carlos?" Sammy demanded.

Uncle Voss said mildly, "I reckon all Diego has on his mind is not being crowded one bit more than the law allows."

Lee had been listening and now he leaned forward. "Is this the Ruiz who lives on Tigre Creek not too far from the Zapata highway?"

Sammy nodded. "You've met?"

"And how! As you know, his land adjoins yours, and it's right at the line I want to drill. I need leases on both areas." He rubbed his forehead. "When I tried to talk to Ruiz, he behaved as if I were the original gringo filibuster."

"He wouldn't lease?" Sammy asked, startled. Like many Border families, the Ruizes just managed to get by. "Why, that's cutting off his nose to spite his own face!"

"Funny how some of us will do that," put in Uncle Voss. Sammy turned quickly to look at him, but his poker face denied any guile. He passed Fran the cloth-covered *tortillas*. "Have you taught school before, Miss Murdoch?"

"Just the required practice teaching. This is my first real job." She glanced through the window at the palms and bougainvillaea. "The country here is so different from Beaumont, my home town. I guess I shouldn't be surprised that my pupils are different too."

Lee, surveying her with approval, asked, "Are most of your kids Latin?"

Holding up five fingers, Fran laughed. "Here's my Anglo portion. Just learning to pronounce the names has taken me hours. But I wouldn't trade this for anything! The children are imaginative and affectionate, not nearly as apt to be bored and unresponsive as some city children. School is full of new, exciting things many of my pupils don't have at home, so they love to come."

"They obey well too," Sammy added. "Goodness knows I'm not a teacher, but usually the kids are easy to handle."

Fran smiled. "I differ with you on one point—you're a natural teacher, Sammy. No amount of education courses can give that instinctive sympathy and understanding. But I do agree that the children respond exceptionally well to discipline. I think"—she laughed and glanced around—

"that it's because they have discipline at home. From what I see, Pop is boss, and the kids know it, though they worship *Mamacita*."

Uncle Voss raised his glass in salute, Lee chuckled, and Sammy sputtered: "Fran! Do you think that's how it ought to be?"

Fran raised her arms in a helpless motion. "Let's be realistic, shall we? In any marriage, usually one person has the final say, though they may discuss matters and each defer sometimes to the other. I don't believe in tyranny on either side. But I think marriages work best when the man generally has the deciding vote. The wife feels she has a husband on whom she can depend. If she always gets her way over his objections, she's often dissatisfied. I've known many girls who have utter contempt for husbands who let women run their lives."

Who would have thought that Fran, charming, intelligent, career-girl Fran, could be such a heretic? When Sammy at last got her dropped jaw back in place, she stared at her friend.

"Would you say a man has a right to choose his work without considering his wife's opinion?"

"Of course he should consider her! But look. He has to spend his life at his job; to him, it's what a house and children are to a woman. If he gave up what he truly wanted to do because his wife objected, he wouldn't be happy. He'd never do what he was capable of doing, and even she would be miserable if she didn't despise him for being so spineless!"

She broke off, took a breath, and laughed. "I sound like 'Women's Rights' in reverse. Pardon my soapbox. But it's better to have the right man than rights, period."

"I don't think so," Sammy murmured. She was thinking of Whit with pain that was worse for coming sudden and undulled.

"Maybe you can have both," Lee suggested with a wink at Uncle Voss. "Besides, if you have to take one and leave the other, it's your free choice."

"Some choice!" Sammy grumbled.

After dinner Fran and Sammy did the dishes, then joined the men in the patio. The late full moon bathed the country in silver-blue light that made it seem like a weirdly beautiful landscape on another planet. From the little hills came a long yipping cry, answered from another point, and soon taken up by a third roamer.

"Wolves?" shivered Fran.

"Coyotes," Sammy explained. "Do you think one of them is Loney, Uncle Voss?"

"Loney doesn't sing when she's this near the ranch. Too shrewd for such capers. That's why she's still loping around while the young smart-alecky ones get caught."

After Fran left, talk shifted to the chances of oil on Tigre Creek. Lee explained that as an independent operator he had all his capital tied up in this venture.

"If I don't hit oil," he said, "I'll have to hire on as a driller with one of the big companies till I get a stake again. Dad and I had our company doing pretty well when I had to go to Korea, but he died while I was gone and operations closed down. I started out fresh, drilled some dry holes, and now I've got to make or break it." He slanted a teasing look at Sammy. "If the formation I have spotted doesn't mean oil, I may toss in with your friend and start doodlebugging, because what they taught me in school wasn't so, and what I've learned isn't either. I think I've got a well!"

"What's the formation like?" Sammy asked.

"Come over tomorrow and I'll show you. Why don't you come too, Mr. Forrester?"

Uncle Voss shook his head regretfully. "I've got to meet the State Game Commission man in Laredo. Some other time? I'm interested, especially since we're leasing to you."

"Come any time." Lee stood up, shaking hands. "Thanks for having me over. The food was great and so was the company." He turned to Sammy. "Ride up Tigre Creek tomorrow and I'll give you lunch. Okay?"

"I'll try." Sammy rose. Even then, Lee was tall and big enough to block out the house lights. Whit was as tall but he was thin, not a man yet. As she told Lee good night, she frowned; what made her think of a thing like that?

Next morning after she and Lupe finished the heavy cleaning, Sammy readied Chispa and headed for Tigre Creek. While she was out that way, she was going to call on Diego Ruiz and talk to him about the English school. She turned off the highway to the brush-grown road she had shown Lee that night he had "lost his shirt."

She loved riding, with the wind tossing back her hair and Chispa's mane. It was like being part of the sun and wind, the magnificent power of the horse. And surely the skies were not this blue anywhere else. The barren, thorny land was made of extremes. White sunlight, a sky so deep a blue it seemed to blaze. You saw the flowers with a gratitude for the mercy of color in the sameness of ashy greens and pale sand. Yellow *retama,* purple sage on frosted stems, even the maroon fruit of the prickly pear.

Wind-gnarled trees had a tortured beauty, and their graceful limbs moved like a dancer's scarves. Sammy had watched them till she found even in the thorns a pattern of severe harmony. This place had healed her spirit after her parents' death. It meant what a home could mean to a person who had never had one.

Today, though, knowing that her wish to stay here had brought on the estrangement from Whit, Sammy found that the spaces did not flow in on her, filling her heart. She was empty. The beauty no longer fulfilled her, and this made her sad and bitter.

Was it that when you grew up places were not enough, you had to be with a man you loved too? But what if the man and the place were widely divided? If you chose one, wouldn't you always regret the other? Whit, in reality, had chosen. He was taking the Air Force. She could go along with that and leave the ranch, or keep the ranch and lose him. Whit had at least a chance of having both her and his career. It just wasn't fair.

Swallowing a lump, Sammy tried to concentrate on the erratic creek she was following. It was a perverse and willful stream, often running dry or flowing underground. Yet, for all its seeming weakness, it had channeled out hunks of the cliffs bordering it. She had only been up this road a few times, but she remembered that one cliff had a smooth, thinly layered face of limestone and shale.

Could that be Lee's formation? Soon it reared straight up from the creek, and on its brush-covered top was a trailer with a canvas extension forming a kind of porch. Recalling the elegance of Lee's low-slung car, she was glad to see a scarred pickup parked beside it.

"Hi!" His voice boomed up at her from the creek.

Glancing down, she saw him eighty feet below at the base of the cliff. A pick, hammer, shovel, and several tools she didn't recognize lay about him. "I'll be right with you," he called. "We'll eat before I show you around because people have starved to death listening to me. I don't want that to happen to you."

Sammy loosened Chispa's saddle and led her down the steep path to water. As she was tying the mare in the shade of a big mesquite, Lee joined her.

"Pretty critter." He stroked the sweat-gleaming reddish hide. "What's her name?"

"Chispa. It means 'Spark.' When do you want Doodlebug to come to work?"

Helping her up the path by pulling on her hand, Lee calculated swiftly, then shrugged. "Oh, it's hopeless trying to figure out when the rig builders and pipe will get here when I haven't decided where to drill. Tell him to come on over Monday. He can be rigging up a cook shack and getting things ready for the crew."

"It's good of you to hire him. Thanks."

"He'll earn his pay." Lee waved her into a canvas chair beneath the awning. "Sit on my porch and cool off. I've got things keeping hot on the stove."

Sammy leaned back, hitching up her slim riding trousers so they wouldn't bind her knees, and enjoyed the breeze on her hot face. In a few minutes Lee came out with a glazed earthenware bowl of stew. He set it on the card table near her. Sammy, already perspiring, watched the steam curl up from the bowl in fascinated horror.

For hot-weather lunches she was strictly a salad-sandwich girl. "The idea," Lee grinned, returning with more stew and a pot of coffee, "is to make the inside of you as cooked as the outside. Equalizes the effects of the weather." He got out cups and silverware and the meal began.

"Dad always said not to eat if you couldn't eat a hot meal," Lee went on. The glint in his eyes made Sammy feel that he was trying to goad her into complaining.

She said sweetly, "Then your father would be very proud of you."

"I'd like to really feed you properly, Sammy. Why don't we go to Nuevo Laredo some night and have dinner and watch the *promenada*?"

Sammy, forgetting the heat, looked up eagerly. "Oh,

that's when the young people walk around the square and flirt."

He nodded. "I used to drive over especially to see it, back when we were drilling north of Laredo. I guess we're too rushed for that kind of courtship, but I like it almost as much as hearing a ruffed grouse drum or watching a peacock spin out his tail."

"You and Fran!" accused Sammy. "There go equal rights again. Female birds are always drabber than the males. It's not fair!"

"They have to impress the ladies somehow. Just like men work hard to attract women."

Sammy came within a breath of snorting. "Now there you're wrong! Who spends hours shopping for pretty things and reducing and exercising and sitting under hair-dryers?"

"Women are supposed to look lovely. It's their life-work."

Jerking so that she almost spilled hot stew down her shirt, Sammy glared at him. "How conceited can you men get? Women aren't dependent on some man for their every cent; we can work and look around too. I suppose you think women should meekly put up with whatever life a man chooses and act as if she likes it!"

"I didn't say it, young lady, but since you bring it up, that's exactly what I think. Unless the woman intends to earn the living while her husband tends the house and kids —poor kids!"

"You're absolutely antique!"

"Men want wives; kids need mothers." Lee's voice stayed teasingly light, but his eyes were uncomfortably intent. "Unless a woman intends to fill those jobs, she shouldn't marry."

As if to dismiss the argument, he rose, taking Sammy's bowl. "Refill?"

"Doesn't it demean you to feed me lunch?" Sammy gibed.

He laughed. "If you're to take what I say to heart, tell me and I'll make it good. I see why Guadalupe calls you Sammy-*Mula!* Come along. I'll show you the formation before you get mad and go home."

Lee showed Sammy how the layers of shale and limestone and sandstone had at one time been subjected to terrific pressure, which had caused them to shift from their normal position and produce a "fault."

"A fault doesn't necessarily mean oil," he explained. "But it does show that this place went though some powerful earth movements of the sort that often produce gas and oil."

Sammy ran her fingers over the marble-smooth surface. Lee told her it had been polished by two rock masses rubbing on each other. Tapping the cliff and gazing along it, Lee gave an exhilarated laugh.

"You know," he said, turning, "what I see in formations like this? I see the brontosaurus lifting his head through those giant prehistoric swamps, and I hear the earth groan and tremble and slowly cover beasts and plants, pressing them into the strata we tap now for oil. That's what oil really is, Sammy, stored-sun energy, trapped underground for thousands of years."

Sammy blinked. *"What?"*

"Come on now, you studied photosynthesis in freshman science! Plants couldn't live without sunlight; they sort of photograph it and make a sugar molecule that can be stored or used. And animal life in the long run depends on plants. So you're really operating on stored sunlight, lady! Don't you feel ethereal?"

"Not especially," Sammy chuckled, glancing down at her very solid arm. She tilted a brightly malicious glance at him. "In your own way, you're as much a dream-chaser as Doodlebug."

He shrugged. "Okay. I hear brontosaurus instead of a dicky bird. Is that bad?"

And Whit hears the jets roar and the props spin, she thought with a stabbing pain. Men don't need women. They just need their darned old careers! Whit was over three hundred miles away, pursuing his. And it was a hot, dusty, suffocating day, with a dark quality in the sunshine all of a sudden. Sammy whirled, hurrying up the bank.

Confusion, shame, and humiliation! She was beginning to cry. At Lee's startled call, "Hey, what's wrong?" she fled blindly.

Her foot gripped a gravel ledge, it crumbled and she fell, grasping wildly at the cliff. Her hands closed on thorns, she screamed and let loose. But she didn't fall far.

Lee had her almost instantly, lifting her up. "Sammy, are you hurt? Let's see your hands."

They stung fiercely and she felt bruised and shaken. She caught her lip with her teeth as Lee opened her hands, even though he was incredibly gentle.

The thorns of the *junco* bush had left long, deep scratches on her fingers and palms, but fortunately none seemed broken off in the flesh.

"I wouldn't have you hurt for the world and this happens! Let's get to camp and I'll fix those hands." In a no-nonsense way he picked her up and at her protest, he said gruffly, "Think I want you to fall again? Get your breath back."

It was luxurious, being carried along this way in strong, sure arms. In spite of his *onza* eyes and worldly experience, he comforted her; with him she was safe, able to relax. For a fleeting second she wondered how it would be to be taken care of like this always, and she realized that since her parents died she had never felt protected or secure. She clung to Los Ladinos as an anchor for her life. But a place, however loved, cannot lift you up and carry you when you hurt yourself.

He placed her in the canvas chair and disappeared into the trailer. He came back with alcohol, iodine, and enough cotton and bandage to outfit an emergency ward, but went at cleaning her scratches so gingerly that Sammy laughed and doused on the antiseptics herself, getting it over fast.

"Goodness, Lee, I thought men were always getting hurt in the oil fields. Besides, I should have looked before I grabbed." She stood up, shaking her hands to dry the iodine and ease the stinging. "I want to see Diego Ruiz, so I'd better go. Thanks for the lunch."

His brows quirked and his sheepish grin confirmed her suspicion that he had served the stew as a joke, to see if she'd fuss. "Any time you're hungry," he invited. "Look, I don't want you to handle those reins with your hands all raw. That greasy leather might infect your cuts. I've got some clean cotton gloves. You wear them."

"I really don't——" Sammy began.

But he was already in the trailer. When he emerged, he poked them over her hands. They reached ludicrously half up her arm. "Keep 'em on," he ordered. "I'll bring your horse over. She seems might frisky. Think you can manage?"

"I can ride Chispa without hands," Sammy said loftily. "She's trained to respond to knee pressure. But if you want to see a wild horse, you'll have to come when the *vaqueros* bring in a coyote dun they've spotted. He's mustang stock and he ought to be as jumpy as a balloon salesman in a cactus patch till I settle him down."

"*You?*"

She frowned. "Sure. I've ridden buckers."

"If I were your Uncle Voss, you wouldn't."

"Then it's lucky for both of us that you aren't. Good-by, Lee. Thanks for telling me about the brontosaurus."

He caught the reins. "Wait a minute. How about that dinner and the *promenada*? There'll be one tomorrow night."

Tomorrow? He didn't waste time, and it was flattering to have a man who had been around a lot seem so attentive. Wishing Whit could hear, Sammy decided quickly.

"I'd love it!"

He smiled up at her. "Fine. I'll stop for you about six."

Riding up the trail, Sammy felt beautiful and alluring and sought-after in spite of her scratches and the cotton gloves. She was, in fact, so taken up with planning what to wear that she had to curb her mind sharply to consider what arguments might convince Diego that the English school was good.

CHAPTER SIX

She found him fixing a hole in his mesquite-limb corral. As if she were just riding by, as she sometimes did, Sammy stopped and they exchanged courteous remarks about the weather and the need for rain.

"I suppose Carlos goes to school this year," Sammy said. "I've met the new teacher. She's very nice."

"*Ay*," said Diego, "I hear that you also teach, Señorita Sam."

Sammy smiled. "That's true." She had known Diego casually for years, but as he watched her with his face as closed and impassive as a stone image's, she didn't know how to proceed. With an appealing motion of her hand she said, "The children like it and it helps them learn faster in school. I wish you'd let Carlos come."

"Is it not enough that we were forced to move, that our people's graves were disturbed, that my village was drowned, that my children will go to school, all by order? They will learn English soon enough." He clamped his sinewy hand on the corral. "I have been ordered and forced and I have learned I cannot withstand the government, but just as surely I will not do anything I am not compelled to do to change the life of my family."

"That's not very friendly, Diego."

He shook his head. "I am sorry. I have respect for you and your uncle, you are *buena gente,* good family. It is that I wish to be left in peace—no more crowding, no more improvements." His face twisted. He made a violent gesture with his hand. "Improvements! Is that what they call it when the old, loved things are drowned, ruined?"

Understanding, yet convinced Diego was, in his hurt, striking out indifferently at all new things whether good or bad, Sammy made a last try.

"Zapata is gone because of Falcón. Yet because of the dam there is water all the long way down the Rio. People can grow crops, and when it doesn't rain they still have drinking water instead of hauling it in the way some had to before."

"It is my town, not theirs, that lies under water."

Defeated, Sammy started to knee Chispa on, but something about the man standing in his brush clearing, lonely and defiant, roused an angry compassion in her. "Diego! How can you make a new life while trying to hang on to the old? It's gone, under the Rio waters. Your home, your life, is here now, and so is that of your children."

"*Es verdad?*" He leaned forward, his corded cheek muscles swelled and his voice vibrated hoarsely. "Listen! Carlos and my younger ones think of Zapata as their home, and they always will! Not the new Zapata, but the town our family helped settle and held title to under grants from the King of Spain. On feast days and on the Day of the Dead I take them there to remember the old ones and our village. That is how it will be, Señorita Sam! You teach English and leave me to teach devotion."

Devotion? Fanaticism was more like it. "I'm sorry for you," Sammy said in a voice that trembled. "I'm sorry that you would rather live in a dark, dead city than walk in the sun. *Adios,* Don Diego."

Turning Chispa, she rode off with a deep sense of failure. There must have been a way to persuade him, but she had only made things worse.

There was a letter from Chuck, following a day after the other because:

> Don Stuart—he's my squadron commander, remember—wants mighty bad to date you for the big Thanksgiving game and dance. I hope you make up with old Whit by then, but if you don't, Don is a nice guy. Also, it won't hurt this fish to have a friend at court in case Ragan keeps on till I knock him flat. Hah!

"Hah-hah!" Sammy echoed aloud. If Chuck had a fight with his first sergeant she would have the most terrific "twin twinge" of all time.

Go with Don? She didn't know. She filed the invitation mentally and sought out Uncle Voss in the patio to tell him about her futile talk with Diego.

"Leave the man be," Uncle Voss said when she finished. "You'll get his back up till he can't change his mind without losin' face. After all, it's his kid and his business."

"Mmm." Swallowing her arguments, Sammy went on to say that Lee had asked her out to dinner.

Uncle Voss scowled, to her shock, and knocked out his pipe. "You shouldn't go, Sam."

"Why ever not? Don't you like Lee?"

"You bet I do. That's just the point." Uncle Voss' gray eyes dwelt sternly on her. "I saw him watching you the other night. He's not interested in dating you to pass the time away. He means business."

"He's a perfect gentleman—" Sammy began.

"Sure, I know that. But when a man that age, a nice one like Lee, dates a girl your age, he has marriage in his mind. Seems to me you should know that when people have opposite notions of what they'll be to each other in future, they are plain headed for trouble."

That hit a raw nerve. "Lee's grown. As long as we have fun together I don't see why I should treat him like poison ivy."

"Think it over, Sam. I think you should at least tell Lee about Whit."

"That we're in cold storage till spring? That sounds ridiculous, Uncle Voss!"

"All the same, it's true. Don't lead Lee down a blind trail. I'm sorry for the way you're all tangled up, honey. I know you're hurt in your pride and heart. But if you and Whit care enough about each other, it'll work out, and if you don't, you sure better find out now. Just try not to get a third person in a lot of trouble because you're mixed up and lonesome."

Sammy turned down her lip. It would be fun to go out with someone attractive and stimulating like Lee. She was sick of going to bed early every night. Interesting as the school was, it left a big gap, a lot of unsatisfied feelings. Still, there was justice in what Uncle Voss said. She nodded.

"All right, I'll tell Lee. But if he wants to take me out anyway, I'm going!"

"So long as he's warned," Uncle Voss said. He squinted up at her with a reproachful grin. "Doggone you, Sam, while my back was turned, you grew into a good-lookin' girl and you sure are behaving like one!"

Sammy and Fran had agreed to spend Sunday afternoon figuring out a better schedule for the English school, so after church Sammy stopped by the house where Fran boarded. With Fran's collection of books and pamphlets, they drove to Los Ladinos and settled at the living-room table, with sandwiches and milk. Uncle Voss had driven Lupe, Martín, and a few other ranch people over to Laredo to celebrate the Mexican Independence Day, the *Grito,* or cry, of Dolores, when the priest, Hidalgo, had made his passionate call to the Mexicans to throw off Spanish rule. The day was enthusiastically honored on both sides of the Rio by people of Mexican descent. The actual holiday was tomorrow but Uncle Voss had taken Lupe and the others today so they could stay overnight and visit relatives, making it a short vacation. Uncle Voss would go back for them Monday night.

"The children keep saying, 'I no have,' " Fran sighed. "It's because of their being used to *no tengo.*' "

"Here's a game that should correct that," Sammy triumphed. She read from the pre-primer manual Fran had acquired. " 'Have the leader ask each child: "Do you have the pencil?" or whatever the concealed object is. The child answers: "No, I do not have the pencil," or, "Yes, I have the pencil." ' "

"That should do it," Fran said. "Most of these games look helpful and fun. One pre-primer teacher told me her children like to take turns giving each other directions like 'Run to the door, tie your shoe,' and so on."

At the end of three hours they had a notebook full of games, songs, lists of the most necessary words, methods of teaching the tricky prepositions, pronouns, and possessives, and several pages of the most common pronunciation errors and ways to correct them.

"This is basic," Sammy mused, stacking up books. "But once the kids know it, they've a good start and we can get more sophisticated. We don't realize it because we're born to it, but English is darned hard to learn."

"That doesn't seem to bother Mr. Ruiz a bit. It's pathetic, Sammy. Carlos watches the other youngsters climb in the car and then he goes home alone. Some of them tease him because they already know more English than he—and that gulf is going to widen."

Sammy pushed at her hair. "I talked to Diego. Talk about a closed mind! He'd hear just as much if he wore earplugs."

"Guess we might as well save our breath." Fran rose and stretched. "That Lee McAllen who was here for dinner— is he a family friend?" She said it with such studied casualness that Sammy felt she had been wanting to ask all day.

"He's new here, hunting oil." Sammy wondered why she found it hard to look at Fran. "Uncle Voss likes him."

"Who wouldn't? Is he married?"

"I certainly hope not! We're going out tonight."

"Oh." Fran gave a quick laugh. "Pardon the inquisition. I'll drink to a fine evening for you when I have my nightly cup of chocolate."

They walked to the house, talking of other things, though the underlying discomfort seemed almost physically tangible. Fran had said enough to show she found Lee intriguing, but Sammy had the date with him. On top of

Uncle Voss's lecture, it made her think that she might be wrong to go out with him when Fran wanted to. But he was, after all, old enough to choose his girl friends. That was the only sensible way to look at it.

These qualms melted into a happy sparkle as Sammy dressed. To go to Nuevo Laredo and see the *promenada* after eating in one of the swank restaurants—why, that was a huge evening, a grown-up evening, particularly with Lee as an escort.

Watching her hair fall gleaming from the brush as she faced the mirror, Sammy slowed the strokes, pondering.

Should she really tell Lee about Whit? Men don't like postmortems, and anyway it was egotistic to assume he cared in the least. Horrible, if he marked her down for a silly child who thought anyone who asked her out had to be warned about falling in love with her.

Unless he said or did something unusual, she wouldn't make a point of Whit, at least not tonight. This decided, she finished brushing. She wore her most glamorous dress, a black cotton eyelet over a satin slip, frosted with crystal necklace and earrings. She had just slipped on her patent pumps when she heard a car stop. Doodlebug must have been on the veranda, because she heard his frail voice alternate with Lee's deep one. She answered the door on the second knock.

Lee whistled, drawing her outside. "Where's your mantilla and comb?" he teased. "I'm not turning you loose on the plaza, that's for sure! See you in the morning, Doodlebug?"

"You bet, Lee! I'm right handy with tools and I'll help any other way I can. Evenin', Miss Sam."

"Hi, Doodlebug. Remember, you can still live at Los Ladinos while you work for Lee."

The old man thrust back his bushy white hair and grinned. "Thanks, but I reckon I'll fort up on Tigre Creek so's to be near my job. *Job.*" He said it lovingly, rolling the sounds on his tongue. His eyes were bright as he looked up. "By gorry, it sure feels good to be back at work!"

In the car, Sammy smiled at Lee. "That's made him ten years younger. He worked around the ranch but never would take money, and the odd jobs he could get just provided a little pocket money. He's a good person, though maybe a little odd."

"Is this a pitch to go easy on him if he tries to convert me to his peach twig?" Lee asked.

She laughed, and they talked about her school and Tigre Creek the rest of the hour-and-a-half drive.

The twin Laredos were divided only by the Rio Grande and the international bridge with its immigration and customs officials on either side. As they passed the Mexican officers and entered Nuevo Laredo, the traffic became pandemonium. Mexican law was based on the Napoleonic Code which assumed guilt till innocence was proven. Because people who got in traffic accidents often had a terrible time settling the mess, many visitors left their cars near the bridge in Texas and walked across the bridge, using a taxi once they were in Mexico.

"The daring shut their eyes and bear down on their horns," Lee said. "Out of deference to you, I'll be conservative and dodge."

This worked, and soon they were sitting in the patio of a supper club, ordering from the white-jacketed waiter. Lanterns magnified the shadows of the swaying palms and three men with guitars were singing their way around the tables.

"Any songs you'd like especially?" Lee inquired.

Enchanted, Sammy clasped her hands under her chin and took a deep breath. "I like them all, Lee. But if they stop here would you ask them to play *'Cielito Lindo'*? I don't care which version, they're all lovely." Lee beckoned and the smiling musicians came over.

"Tell them what you want to hear," he said and gave the leader a bill.

So while Sammy and Lee worked through *guacamole*, rice with chicken, melted cheese sauce with crisp *tostadas*, chilled mangoes and coffee, they had music, in the language that enthralled Sammy, took her back to the golden days of Don Isidro.

> "On the morning you were born,
> Were born the flowers . . .
> . . . From the stars in the sky
> I'd like to take down two.
> One with which to greet you,
> The other to say *adiós*."

The guitars throbbed on, while the strong sweet voices crested into *"Cielito Lindo,"* "Beautiful Little Heaven."

"Only on Sunday I see your face,
When you go to Mass in the morning . . ."

Lee said, "Hard on a boy, to only see his girl that way!" Sammy didn't answer. She was following the next tune, one she hadn't asked for, one she hadn't known:

"Do not look for me along the highway, *mi bien.*
Look for me along the short cut . . .
And there you will find me singing, *mi bien,*
About the love I had for you."

Whit wouldn't look for her along the highway or the short cut or any road at all. The wind in the palms, the soft light, the poignant songs; a silent weeping rose in Sammy till her throat ached and her lips fixed in a numb smile.

Lee seemed to sense her change of mood. He called for the check and they left for the plaza.

From across the street they watched the gay young people drift around the city square while chaperones and older folk sat on the benches and a band played. The men walked down the center of the broad walk, and on either side of this aggressive column moved demurely flirtatious girls.

"Smiles and glances—once in a while a smuggled note," said Lee. "Do you like that style of courtship, Sammy?"

"I would have if I'd had the chance." But that, no matter how decorous, was the last thing she felt capable of watching right now. After a decent length of time she glanced obviously at her watch.

"Ready to go?" Lee asked.

She tried not to sound too relieved. "Whatever you think. It is quite a drive." He nodded and they walked back to the car. After he paid a uniformed man for watching it, he paused before he helped Sammy in.

"Bottom fell out of the evening," he said without rancor. "What happened, Sammy? Why?"

"You're imagining things! I had a splendid time."

"Yes. That's why you almost cried during the songs, isn't it?"

She looked away from him. "The songs were so pretty they hurt."

"So are you, but I don't cry about it."

Lee crying? The idea was so ridiculous that Sammy had to laugh. "I should hope not!"

He shrugged, got in the car. They passed customs and Sammy shot a worried look toward him.

His jaw made a black angle against the night. The light from the dashboard touched his fingers, and the careless, easy way he handled the wheel made her acutely aware of the difference in their age and experience.

Was he angry at her for spoiling the evening? It wasn't fair to repay a man's time and effort with gloom. Miserably she gripped her purse and stared out the window.

She wouldn't do this again! No more dates, absolutely, till she could behave, keep Whit out of mind. She doubted if the memory of her interfered with *his* fun. Lee's voice tugged at her.

"Hey, come back inside."

When she didn't turn, the car left the road. Calmly, deliberately, Lee clicked off the ignition.

CHAPTER SEVEN

As Sammy turned in surprise, Lee sat back, folding his arms. "Okay." His voice wasn't resentful, but it had a coolly businesslike note that gave her an idea of how he could sound in discussing leases or poor work from a crew. "Let's have it. Who sent the evening on the rocks?"

"I—I don't know."

"Yes, you do."

Smarting, Sammy clenched her fists. "I'm sorry! I'm truly ashamed! I fouled up your party and I shouldn't have gone. I never will again. Now—please, *please* take me home!"

"When you talk." He settled himself more comfortably. "You were running away from something the other day when you fell on the cliff. Tonight, in another way, you ran. I'm a patient individual, but I don't intend to have you going off from me all the time."

She looked straight ahead. He lit a cigarette. The knowledge that he was sitting there watching her ate at Sammy's nerves.

"You can't stay here all night!" she cried.

"I won't have to. I reckon you'll tell me inside an hour. You can't keep still longer than that."

Oh, couldn't she? He blew smoke rings. Sammy simmered. When her blood reached a fine, steady boil, she faced him. All she cared about was escaping. Lee couldn't like her after this anyway.

"If you just have to know, I was thinking about a boy I used to go with. I—I thought we'd be married, only I guess we won't. Now please take me home!"

After a moment Lee asked in an emotionless tone, "What happened? Do you still love him?"

"Yes." Sammy's lip trembled. "But he's going to make the Air Force a career. In fact, he almost told me I could take it or leave it."

"Have you decided which it's going to be?"

Sammy couldn't help it. She put her face in her arms against the seat back and wailed. "No! And quit asking things!" Lee stayed quiet till Sammy got herself under control. Straightening her skirt, she blew her nose without trying to be jaunty, and swallowed. "I suppose you ought to know about Whit. He's a senior at A & M. We're not writing or dating till we're sure how we feel about each other. I meant to tell you—only not in such an uncivilized way."

Lee chuckled and it was somehow very comforting. "Don't take it so hard. It helps to admit your feelings once every decade or so, don't you think?"

"I'd far rather not."

"It is painful. But you have to see your trouble before you can whip it. If your little Latin kids insisted that they could already speak fine English and needn't learn, would they solve anything?" His voice took on a grim edge. "Your problem is this boy. Whose idea, if I may be inquisitive, was this cooling-off period?"

"His." Sammy sniffed. "He knows I abominate the Air Force so he's giving me a lovely choice. Los Ladinos or him."

"Heaven knows I don't want to talk for another guy, Sammy, but this Whit seems to have played straight with you."

Men! They hung together, all right. Even Chuck and Uncle Voss had tacitly sided with Whit.

"You don't understand," Sammy denied, shaking her head vehemently. "We went steady right up till this fall. We used to talk about raising horses and the ranch . . . I shouldn't have counted on it, perhaps, after Whit got interested in flying, but I went on thinking our plans were the same—not thinking, really. It seemed natural. Then the night before he left for school, he told me he'd signed a five-year contract and that he wanted to stay in as a career."

"Why the deep rancor at the Air Force?"

"It's not rancor. I've no desire to go back to being a human tumbleweed, that's all. My father was a career officer. I grew up moving all the time. When he and mother were killed, it was the end of my world. With them gone, there was nothing, not even a home, a place we belonged to. Then Uncle Voss brought Chuck and me to Los Ladinos." Sammy thought back, phrasing it slowly. "It was like going back to a stronger time when people had pride of place and belonging. I felt as if I were part of the ranch and the country. It was here before me and will be after me and I want to make Los Ladinos into what it used to be, raise fine horses, and give Martín and Vicente pride in what we do."

She could see Lee's profile briefly as he lit a new cigarette. He spoke slowly. "Maybe your Whit wants the Air Force as strongly as you want to stay here. Do you expect him to make a sacrifice that you won't?"

"That," said Sammy, "is what I'm trying to decide. Only if there's any sacrificing done, I'll do it. Whit is definite. The wild blue for him and I can suit myself."

"It seems to me that if a girl loved enough to marry, she'd be ready to take whatever went with it."

"Sure," Sammy returned dourly. "Only men are supposed to eat their cake and have it too."

Lee hooted merrily. He gave her cheek a pat and put the car on the road. "You're a truthful gal, Sammy. I doubt you gave your lad the subtle treatment?"

"What was there to be subtle about? *He* was plain enough."

Slanting a long look at her, Lee said, "I shouldn't tell you this. But if you want to jab that dumb cadet into action you shouldn't sulk down here in the chaparral. It's easy to resist unseen temptations, but oh brother! When the beautiful things materialize!"

"Why are you concerned about all this? I thought you were—were———" Trapped into sounding conceited, Sammy floundered till Lee took up the sentence.

"Interested in you? I am. And I want the deck clear for action. That means I don't want this Whit dangling in your mind like a skeleton in a closet. I, dear lady, am all for making him declare himself. I don't go along with this deep-freeze policy!"

"Mmm. Maybe you think I should go to the Thanksgiving game with this other Aggie who invited me? Make Whit jealous?"

"Sure, make him squirm." Lee's eyes flicked toward Sammy. "Pardon my curiosity, young lady; but you haven't dated a lot, have you?"

Sammy flushed. "Does it show?" Defensively she added, "I went out with quite a few boys before we came here, but that was when I was younger. Whit and I have gone steady since I was a sophomore in high and he was a freshman at A & M."

"Then it's about time you had a change," Lee admonished her. "You need to study other members of the species! Learn about men and how to bring 'em back alive. You can begin with me, of course."

He said this in such a smug tone that Sammy had to laugh. "But, Lee———"

"Don't argue. I know your dreadful secret and if I still like your company, that's my lookout, isn't it?" When she stared dazedly at him, he went on in his half-bantering, half-serious way. "Look, I'm offering to teach you how to make men jump through hoops, roll over, and play dead. Not every girl gets a chance like this! They learn the hard way from men who are interested in anything but teaching them how to handle them. I'm a lion, come to teach the tamer."

"No, you're an *onza*."

"A which?"

She explained and said with a little shiver, "The night I met you, I thought you were one. I almost stepped on the gas."

"I'm glad you didn't."

"So'm I," she said truthfully. Lee made life a good deal pleasanter, even when he teased or acted bossy.

"Then may I enroll you in my seminar in male psychology?"

Tempted but trying to be fair, Sammy frowned. "I don't think I should, Lee. You'd have more fun going with girls who———"

"Were interested primarily in me, not an Aggie? Don't worry. I'll look out for myself. Would it be fun for you?"

"Oh, yes! But . . ."

"Then you're enrolled. I'll come visit your English class tomorrow. And tonight you accept that invitation to A & M, hear? The sooner that cadet is settled, the better pleased I'll be!"

It was still six weeks till the big game. Prayerfully hoping that seeing her with Don would make Whit forget his no-date decision, Sammy wrote Chuck, saying if Don invited her to the game she would go. School wouldn't meet during the holiday so she wouldn't be leaving her English pupils in the lurch.

As she sealed the letter she caught herself holding it and thinking of Lee. It was certainly confusing! He was telling her how to intrigue Whit though he, Lee, seemed to like her. Perhaps being older and used to making up one's mind to hard things did that. Made it preferable to have an impossible dream sabotaged at once rather than let it drag on and die slowly. Sammy envied his strength, the gay manner in which he dared a loss.

She was fearful. Break off clean with Whit, forgo the slight chance he might think of some way to let her keep her ties with Los Ladinos? She knew, with some anger, that she'd wait and hope.

Lee came by next day just as the children, following Sammy's lead, were acting out a song, holding their hands to their foreheads to simulate big teddy-bear ears.

> "Little teddy bear can sit and stand and walk,
> Little teddy bear can sit and stand and walk,
> Little teddy bear can sit and stand and walk,
> And hurry to the door."

As the children saw the tall blond man, they stopped short of the door, squealing. Lee grinned at them and handed Sammy a box of candy bars.

"A donation to higher learning," he whispered and sat down by Fran, who smiled and made room.

Sammy turned, perhaps more abruptly than necessary, went to the blackboard, and drew a not especially elegant doll. "Rudi," she summoned, "color the dress and tell us what color it is."

Eyes glowing, Rudi chalked in red flowers on a blue ground. "The dress is blue. The flowers are red." Wiping his hands, he smoothed them down his blue jeans, looked proudly about, and took his seat.

"Good!" Sammy applauded. "Now, Juana, color the hair and tell us about it."

The hour passed with practice and games, ending with Lee's distribution of the candy. After Fran left with the townward children, Lee helped Sammy straighten the room.

"You've got a good thing here," he said sincerely. "The kids are having a ball, but they're learning too."

Sammy nodded, pleased. "At first I was terribly scared. It seemed like so much to bite off without any training. But it does seem to be helping." She gave the room a last check and looked up at him. "You've never been properly introduced to the ranch. Have time to look around?"

"You bet. After all, it must be some place to rival one of those Aggie seniors, boots and all." When she stared to see if he were teasing, he spread wide, calloused palms. "Honest, when I went to school at Texas University I had a hard time keeping a girl. Durned Aggies stole 'em. Let's see the rancho!"

She took him on the guided tour around the buildings and corrals. Granary, old smithy now used only for shoeing horses, the *campo santo,* or holy ground, where old Don Isidro drowsed under warm earth, the small orange grove with its border of banana trees and giant palms. Martín was in the big barn mending harness and she introduced Lee to him.

Martín condescended to speak English and so she knew the old *vaquero* had judged Lee and found him a man. As she led him through the front part of the building where the saddles and gear were hung Lee stroked a braided rawhide rope tied to one of the cantles.

"Looks like this could hold the meanest horse that ever bucked."

"If the right man had hold of one end." Sammy moved

to her saddle and slipped off the rawhide riata Martín himself had made for her. "Chuck ropes a lot better than I do and of course all the *vaqueros* can do rings around either of us. I could show you a few of the throws, though, if you like."

Lee bowed. "To watch you do anything, *lindísima,* is pleasure."

Sammy laughed to hide the quick rush of color to her face. "You've learned some Spanish," she accused.

"The better to court you with, my dear."

Disconcerted, for Lee's jokes were usually serious underneath, Sammy stepped out into the corral, shielding her eyes from the bright sun.

"Now if I were on horseback I'd show you the way Los Ladinos people rope with the end tied to the saddlehorn. It is a kind of pride to rope and hold on, no getting loose even if you're dragged through the thickets. Martín and the men scorn the dally users, the ones who give the rope a turn around the saddlehorn and use it as a snubbing post. Mostly here in the brush we use a short riata like this, about forty feet long, and we tie fast."

"Yes, ma'am," said Lee.

She glanced around quickly to see if he were making fun, but though he was grinning, it was in an approving, delighted way. So she threw the big-as-all-outdoors Blocker loop, and the small Bird's-Nest which obligingly settled on the post she was throwing at.

"This *peal,*" she explained, casting it out, "would never put 'socks' on the animal as it's supposed to, catching each of the back feet in one loop of the figure-eight. But I can throw a fair *mangana.*" She demonstrated this underhand throw used mostly to catch horses by snaring their front feet, and held out the rope to Lee. "Want to try?"

He shook his head. "Martín's watching. By the time he saw me get tangled good and proper, he wouldn't want me degrading Los Ladinos by coming here. You keep the honors."

"Sometime you'll have to see the *vaqueros* throw on horseback. It's beautiful. The boys play with lariats the way Chuck used to play with guns. Lupe's always having to scold Rudi for roping the roosters and catching their tail feathers." She put the rope back on the saddle where it was always carried. When she turned, Lee's eyes were on her with an expression that made her move back against the saddle.

All he said was, "Did you write about the A & M game last night?"

"Yes." She hesitated, wanting desperately to ask, yet afraid of sounding foolish. "Lee, I don't understand. It seems so strange that you——"

His big hand propelled her about and back into the sun outside. "I can let go, Sammy, if I have to. I'd rather do it early than late, that's all. Don't you feel better, no matter what your decision, once you've acted and it's settled?"

Sammy looked at the white dust. "I don't know. I—I hate to lose things, Lee, I don't know if I can let go."

"When you're clutching things tight to keep them, aren't you made prisoner by that very act? You're held, too, and you can't reach for any new thing till your hands are empty." Sammy was quiet, knowing he was right but helpless against her feelings. Lee got in his car. "I'm tied up the rest of the week, but I'll call you this Friday if it's all right."

"Fine." Sammy managed to smile and wave. But she wondered as she went to the house if Lee thought she was a coward. Well, wasn't she? What else could he think? And why, when she loved Whit, should it matter this deeply, Lee's opinion of her?

October ended, the sameness of the year unruffled yet by a norther, the skies as blue as those of June and the wind almost as warm though it cooled at night. Sammy enjoyed her several dates with Lee and rode in the little hills in her spare time, trying to catch a glimpse of the coyote dun, but he seemed to have turned into the gray-washed yellow sandstone, or perhaps he was only a ghost of one of Don Isidro's mustangs.

Don Stuart had written, definitely inviting her to the Thanksgiving festivities, and she'd answered yes. Chuck's letters were few and laconic. He never mentioned Ragan and that worried Sammy; neither did he mention Whit, and that annoyed her. She might have broken up with Whit, but her twin ought to *know* she wanted to hear what he was doing—if he was winning honors, if he had another girl . . .

Lee hadn't begun drilling yet. There had been a delay with the tools, and besides, he still felt the best location was slightly over on Diego Ruiz's land. Diego refused stubbornly to lease. He said that no oil would be found and that the only result would be to pollute the water his goats drank.

"Anyhow," grumbled Doodlebug one day as Sammy rode by the camp to see how things were going, "my peach twig gets a real strong pull up the draw from this fault, quite a bit further in on Ruiz's place. That's where we ought to drill."

Lee grimaced. "Oldtimer, I have to drill where I think the oil is. Besides, Ruiz doesn't intend to even let me do that. When the tools come, I guess I'll locate as close to the boundary as possible, and hope for the best."

Sammy had coffee with them and rode south toward the Rio. This was November 2, the Day of the Dead. On midnight of the first, the Mexicans believed their dead began coming back to visit and be happy with their families. It was a little like Hallowe'en, but with no fear attached to the feasts and celebrations. Some people took food and gifts to the cemetery for their loved ones, and had picnic lunches. Though the idea of it prickled Sammy's scalp, she could understand that to people who accepted the Day as calmly as she did Christmas, it would be comforting to believe that once each year you were with your loved dead. It made death less final, kept it from being a farewell.

Would Diego have his family at the lake, as he had said he would, to spend the day with the spirits of those who once lived in old Zapata?

Sammy herself had a strange feeling about her parents. She didn't, couldn't, think that all their energy and gay courage had left the earth. She believed they were part of the wind and light that touched her every day, that they belonged to the sun and lived in her also, especially when she did something that would have pleased them or that they would have done had they been there.

But this made her better able to live. She didn't see how Diego's bitter clinging to the past could help him or his children. Sammy reached the lush grass that grew around the lake.

It was the rim of sundown, red in all the west. She could almost see the old town beneath the water, hear its church bell and the women calling their children. If the spirits had come back today, what would they think of finding their village under water?

Perhaps to them it didn't matter. They might walk their streets as easily now as they had once moved on land. A sudden wail caused Sammy to jump. Chispa went into a fidget.

Sure her ears were playing tricks, Sammy quieted the mare and listened. The cry came again. A cry of terror and appeal.

Spinning Chispa, Sammy raced along the lake toward the sound. Coming down a gentle slope, she saw the Ruiz's ancient car, and blankets spread for a picnic.

People were splashing into the water. Far beyond them floated a raft, but no one was on it.

"Mi niño, mi niño!" Diego's wife screamed, holding a small baby in her arms as she stood waist-deep in the lake.

A hand flung out of the water near the raft, clutched frantically at the air, disappeared. Splashing into the water, Sammy cried to Diego who was pulling off his boots, "Oh hurry!"

His strained face swung up. "I can't swim," he said hoarsely. He started to plunge on out.

"Wait!" Sammy called. There was no use in his drowning too. "Maybe I can swim Chispa out there. Who is it?"

"Carlos," moaned the mother. *"Ay, por Dios——"*

Chispa refused the water for a maddening instant; then, slowly, reluctantly, she moved in. If her hoofs struck the boy it would mangle him, and Sammy couldn't see far under the roiled dark water. If only she knew how to swim! Her frantic glance fell on the rawhide riata.

Securing it hastily to the horn, she held to it, keeping the surplus looped in her hand. When Chispa was close to where the hand had showed, Sammy knew she didn't dare ride closer. She took a deep breath and slipped out of the saddle. Holding the rope and tie straps with her right hand, she propelled herself away from Chispa, reaching, hunting . . . A black head broke the water, bare inches from her hand.

"Carlos!" she shouted, gasping, but he had gone back under, and she felt his body touch against her arm.

Catching at him, she hauled his head up, pulled herself back to Chispa's side. "Lie still, Carlos," she panted. It was impossible to get into the saddle with the boy in her one arm while the other hand strained to keep its grasp on the saving rope. She did manage to work the rope under

Carlos' arms so that some of the weight was spared her. She tugged at the reins looped over the saddlehorn till Chispa turned slowly and swam back to the shore where Diego and his wife and the others were standing as far as they could into the lake.

In minutes Carlos was cuddled and wrapped in blankets. His teeth were chattering, his lips were blue, but his dark lashes raised from soft black eyes and he grinned at Sammy, reaching for her, leaving a wet kiss on her cheek.

Señora Ruiz patted Sammy's hand in an ecstasy of gratitude. *"Gracias, señorita. Mil gracias!"*

"It was Chispa," Sammy said, smiling at the pretty young woman who couldn't have been much older than Fran. Seeing the puzzled look in her eyes, Sammy added, *"De nada.* It's nothing." She pushed back Carlos' dripping hair. *"Adiós, hombrecito.* Be well swiftly!"

Diego, hugging his child, looked her square in the eye. "Señorita Sam! It is only courtesy for Carlos to learn the tongue of the one who saved him. He will be at your school tomorrow."

Sammy almost fell over. Grasping the saddlehorn, she recovered enough to say, "Thank you, Don Diego. He will be welcome." Answering the tide of good-byes and good wishes, she rode away.

Happy as she was about Carlos, a reaction from fright and the cold water had set in. She shivered, soaked to the skin and unable to dry out because the sun had gone down and the breeze was cool.

It was silly to think of it now that everything was all right, but she kept seeing Carlos' despairing hand and thinking how awful it would have been if he had drowned. The way home had never been so long. For once she wished Uncle Voss would come looking for her, preferably with hot coffee and a change of clothes, but of course he couldn't know what had happened. She was riding in a daze of chill and discomfort when Lee's voice came from the side of the road.

"Sammy! Why, for the love of mud, are you hunched up like that?"

"Mud's v-very apt," she said between clicking teeth. "We've been in the lake." While she went on talking, Lee took the reins, leading Chispa toward the trailer on the cliff.

"Dry clothes and hot soup for you," he ruled. "Then I'll take you home in the car. Doodlebug can ride Chispa for you."

"Oh, it's not worth all that trouble!"

"I think it is." Lifting her from the saddle in spite of her protests, he carried her into the trailer. "Put the soup back on, Doodlebug! We've got company."

"All this fuss—" Sammy argued, starting up from the bunk where Lee had deposited her.

He pushed her back with one hand and worked off her wet boots, squinting upward. "An extra psychology lesson," he said solemnly. "Never tell a man you can get along without his help. Very poor tactics." He got socks and pajamas out of a drawer. "These will swallow you, but they're dry."

Leaving her to change, he roamed off to help Doodlebug. As Sammy gratefully rid herself of the clammy jeans and shirt, she took a deep sniff of the teasing soup smell and wrestled her way into the big garments. How nice it was, sometimes, to be taken care of!

CHAPTER EIGHT

Carlos was waiting with the ranch children next afternoon to hop into the station wagon. Except for extremely solemn eyes, he looked none the worse for his close escape. After English class he came to Sammy.

"*Mi madre*—she *quiere* learn the English. She—*quiere* tell *gracias,* Señorita Sam." After this speech, delivered with the dignity of a medieval cavalier, he reached up and hugged Sammy explosively.

"I heard all about it," Fran said as he ran off. "You're the gilded gal of the Rio now. If I'd done it, I wouldn't have had to stand anyone in the corner for the rest of the year."

"All I did was hang onto Carlos and the saddlehorn while Chispa swam," demurred Sammy.

Fran laughed. "However it was, our last holdout is now in class. *Salud,* Sammy!" Sammy slid under the wheel, starting the cavalcade to the ranch. She'd have a lot to tell

Chuck on Thanksgiving, things that were too complicated to detail in letters.

Her thoughts jumped to Whit before she could check them. When he saw her with Don, would he care? Or would he leave things to rock along till summer? Just how far apart, really, had they grown? She wished the future were settled, but like a person balancing fine crystal, she was afraid to move for fear of breaking everything.

The Thanksgiving trip would require a new dress. Surrounded by sketches and pattern magazines, Sammy was in a deep study, when Lee walked in. "Oh, good." Sammy shoved the magazines at him. "You can give me the man's point of view." He put his hand on the magazines and wrinkled his brows at her.

"Haven't you listened to me at all these past two months?"

"Of course, but——"

His finger on her lips hushed her. "Then you should know it's you the boy is interested in. He shouldn't notice your dress except as a background. Just as he shouldn't think, 'Her lipstick's a pretty color,' but 'Gosh, will she let me kiss her tonight?' Understand?"

"Some dresses are better backgrounds than others. See this one with the lace overskirt and décolleté? I think it'd be lovely. Sort of a portrait effect."

"Sure, if you plan to pose for your future descendants. But if you want to look like you and feel like a human being, try this." He brought his blunt finger down on a slim dress with soft lines and a bateau neckline.

"It's terribly plain. For a party, I think I should——"

"Wear what suits, and this does. You have fine bones, Sammy, and a beautiful way of moving, sort of spirited and free like your mustangs. It's an outdoorsy kind of grace, a wind-sun style; doesn't fit with minuets and powdered hair." He shrugged, crossing his arms. "Do what you want. But with your tan and your dark hair, you'd knock 'em out in gold velvet. Also, being practical, it won't rip. That's the sad experienced voice of a man who's accidentally stepped on his share of flimsy hems and stoles, the tearing sounds of which were more horrible than any noise I ever heard in battle!"

"Mmmm." Sammy glanced from one sketch to the other.

"I'll think about it. How does the future Number One oil well progress?"

Lee grinned. "It's time you asked! My rig builder showed up today, my tools are due in the morning, and the morning after you pulled Ruiz's kid out of the lake, Ruiz came over and talked lease. He did it, he said, because you like me, and all he has is yours to command. Still and all, he wasn't too unhappy with the lease money I forked over."

"Oh, I hope you bring in a good well," Sammy exclaimed. "Won't Diego get royalties if you do?"

"Yes, the landowner's percentage. He doesn't think anything will come of the well, of course; he's a pessimist about things. But his agreeing to the lease may be the best gift he could possibly make his children." Lee stood up. "We're sinking a test well as quickly as we can, and I'll be busy as a kid on an anthill. But I want to see your new dress and engrave my face on your memory right before you go up to Aggieland."

"Come over any chance you get," Sammy invited. "Let us know how the drilling goes." She watched him go out to his car with a lonely feeling.

These past weeks she'd grown used to his company. From Doodlebug's talk, she knew that bringing in a well was a fatiguing job, often keeping the driller at the rig nights as well as days.

Wouldn't it be wonderful if the oil came in on the boundary and gave Los Ladinos some royalties too? With a substantial hunk of cash, Uncle Voss might feel like turning the watermelon patches back to grazing land.

Between English school and getting new clothes for the football week end, Sammy didn't have much time to miss Lee. She found a beautiful gold velvet, the color of turning leaves, in San Antonio. With careful fittings, Lupe sculpted a form-following dress that Sammy loved, both on and off. Lee had been right; she belonged in this style. It kept her personality free and uninhibited.

She shopped till she found the exact shade of antique bronze in pumps and a bag, added gold velvet gloves that crushed about the wrist. Her mist-green suit with its matching sweater and a new golden-beige one completed her outfit. She didn't want to carry more than she had to since she would be the house guest of Don Stuart's air science instructor, Captain Halley.

Football games filled the motels and hotels near College Station to overflowing. Often instructors would invite their students to quarter dates in their homes. As Whit's guest, Sammy had appreciated this hospitality a number of times. She tried, as she got her things ready to go, not to compare this trip to those former ones when Whit had been waiting to meet her.

She was going as Don's date, they were going to have fun. If Whit had a change of heart, if he found he didn't enjoy watching her with another boy, he could say so. That was what this separation was for, wasn't it? To learn how they really felt?

Anyway, she needed to talk to Chuck. The "twin twinges" lately had come thick and fast. Chuck hadn't written in two weeks, but in her last letter she'd told him to be packed and ready to come back with her for the Thanksgiving vacation. She'd see him at the barrack before Don took her to the Halley's.

Lee came by the day before she left. He had lost weight and was burned even browner, but he had the driving, zestful air of a man absorbed in his chosen work.

"I came to see that dress," he said, taking her hands and whirling her around. "But most of all to see the girl!"

She laughed breathlessly. How good it was to have him here again! She'd forgotten how warm and strong his hands were, how deep and pleasant his voice. "How is the well?" she asked.

"Call it the Sammy-*Mula* Number One," he corrected, turning to include Uncle Voss. "Well, there's gas bubbling in the waste ditch. That's a good sign, since gas and oil are often found together. But we've had our troubles—breakdowns in the equipment, tool-pusher who can't stay sober, the usual vexations."

"Suppose it just proves to be gas," suggested Uncle Voss. "Would it have any value?"

"Sure. The gas company could use it in their pipeline. Of course an oil strike is what I'm after." He rubbed his eyes. For the first time Sammy noticed they were bloodshot, and she frowned in concern.

"You're not getting enough rest, Lee. Why don't you stay here tonight and sleep in peace?"

He shook his head. "Can't do that. I should be at the rig this minute. Model the dress. That'll revive me."

When she came back down the hall fifteen minutes later in
the golden dress and bronze shoes, Lee stood perfectly still
and watched till she was only a few feet away.

Then, stepping across the space, he took her face between
his palms. Deftly, lightly, he kissed her.

"I don't know what color your lipstick is," he said. "All
I thought was, 'Will she let me kiss her?' the way I told you
a man should." He bowed till she could have placed her
hand on his crisp hair. "I give you an A for this term, and I
look forward to the next." Uncle Voss filled his pipe and
glanced up with a hint of wistfulness.

"You're a dream, Sam. In all my life I only saw one other
girl as pretty."

Sammy pouted. "That's no way to pay a compliment!
Who was she?"

"Your mother, when she came to the Senior Ring Dance
with me and met my kid brother. He was her age, a freshman."

Unbelievingly Sammy gazed at your uncle. *"You* dated
Mother? Before she knew Dad?"

"Yes, ma'am." He puffed out a cloud of smoke and
cocked a mock-indignant eyebrow at her. "I didn't always
act like Methuselah and chase Loney through the brush, you
know!"

Lee said good-by then, and Sammy waved to him from
the veranda. She stood there awhile, wondering, shaken.

Mother and Dad hadn't always been together as she remembered them. They'd met and loved and chosen when
they weren't much older than she—and at the same school
where she was going tomorrow. If mother had gone to the
Ring Dance, that meant she had been an extra-special girl
of Uncle Voss'.

Had there been trouble when she picked the younger
brother? And had she dreaded service life, preferring the
familiar pattern of her home town in Louisiana? Sammy
drifted back to her room to change. She wished she could
talk to her mother. Lee could tell her how men felt, but
Sammy needed to know about women, have herself, her
mixed-up, contrary longings, explained.

College Station was already filled with ex-Aggies and
visitors down a day early to yell practice and the annual

bonfire. Don Stuart rushed out when Sammy stopped at the barrack.

"We're still hauling trees for the fire," he panted, leaning in. "I'll take you to Halley's and then I've got to get out to the woods. You can leave your station wagon here."

"Where's Chuck?" Sammy asked, getting out while Don extracted her suitcase.

"He's out hauling trees with the rest of the boys." Don's gray eyes lit up as he smiled down at her. "Sorry to have to take right off, but I'll be back to pick you up before supper, and then we'll go to yell practice." Opening the door to his green convertible, Don scanned her again, nodded in pleased satisfaction as if an opinion had been reaffirmed. "I sure am happy you came!"

Mrs. Halley was young and pretty, with ash-blonde hair and hazel eyes. She had a boy eight years old, and a girl of three. She greeted Sammy with cordial friendliness and showed her to the guest room.

"Just come and go as you like, Sammy. Of course you're invited to breakfast."

"It's nice of you to have me," Sammy answered, already planning to accompany her bread-and-butter note with an extra-pretty hostess gift.

Mrs. Halley dimpled. "Jim and I like to have you girls. We feel we're repaying the instructors who let me stay with them while Jim was going here and I was at Baylor."

"Captain Halley graduated from A & M?"

"Ten years ago. That's why we were so pleased with this assignment. Especially after Labrador."

The very word brought gooseflesh out on Sammy. "Labrador! Didn't you hate it?"

"Sometimes. But we've separated often enough to make the North Pole look fine so long as we could be together."

That was how Mother had felt. Slowly Sammy began to unpack. She didn't feel that way about Whit yet, and wasn't sure that she wanted to. Did that mean she wasn't in love enough for marriage?

Don came by at dusk. They had dinner at one of the restaurants on Highway Number 6. "I want to see Chuck," Sammy reminded him. "Aren't they through with the bonfire yet?"

"It's all ready to light," Don assured her. "I told Chuck

you were here. You'll see him at yell practice." After a moment's hesitation the blond squadron commander added,
"I hate like the dickens to tell you this, but Chuck was up
before the Cadet Court for breach of discipline. He's restricted to the campus for the holidays." He paused. "He's
taking it as a personal insult."

Sammy stiffened. She remembered from Whit's talk that
the court was a tribunal made up of cadet officers to deal
with infractions of the Articles of the Cadet Corps. They
recommended a sentence which was enforced, however,
only upon approval of the Commandant, the state-appointed
supervisor of the Corps.

"Did you sit on the Court?" Sammy demanded.

Don shook his head. "No. But if I had, I'd have gone
along with the sentence. Look, Sammy, if your brother
wants to be an Aggie, he has to accept the discipline. He
can't tell his first sergeant to shut up and get out of his
room."

"Oh, he told Ragan that?" Sammy almost smiled in spite
of her distress, but then she sobered. Unbridled Chuck, used
to his own free way, what would become of him, if he was
in this trouble after only two and a half months?

The metal buttons on Don's shirt glinted as he leaned forward. He was evidently finding his Corps position something
of a load, but a load he intended to carry with credit. "Talk
to Chuck, Sammy. Ragan's overbearing, but Chuck has a
real tempting chip on his shoulder. He can't seem to understand that the officers whose orders he resents had to take
them too, when they were fish."

"I'll talk to him," Sammy promised. "But—oh, darn!
We'd counted on having him home a few days."

"I'm sorry."

Sammy laughed at Don's guarded tone. "Don't worry,
I'm not going to ask you to let him off." A sudden thought
struck her. "Was Whit Granger on the Court?"

"Why, yes," said Don, "I think he was. But as I said, any
cadet would've had to give the same recommendation.
Whit's got a mighty high notion of duty anyway."

"Yes," nodded Sammy. "Of that I'm sure!"

A huge crowd was gathering for the bonfire—townspeople, visitors, students. The campus streets were jammed
with freshmen and sophomores going to yell practice, while

seniors and juniors exercised their privilege of using the sidewalks. Don parked at the first possible place, and they walked toward the drill field in the brisk fall weather.

"How high is the bonfire this year?" Sammy asked.

"Sixty feet. It would've been higher but some boys from Texas University got past the guard night before last and tore down part of it before the cadets ran 'em off."

The week before the game was spent making the vast woodpile. When not in class, the Aggies were out chopping trees and hauling them in big trucks to the drill field. Don and Sammy found standing places just as the band swung onto the drill field, playing "The Aggie War Hymn." Atop the tepee-shaped structure was hoisted a shack symbolizing the Texas University teahouse. Cadets locked arms around the stack as it was doused with aviation fuel.

The blaze exploded high into the black night, lighting up the drill field, the excited faces. Guest speakers were introduced and made their talks over the public-address system. Then the yell leaders led the pep rally, while the band played the songs. Sammy joined in on "The War Hymn." She'd sung it often enough:

> "Hulabaloo, Caneck, Caneck!
> Hulabaloo, Caneck, Caneck!
> Good-by to Texas University,
> So long to the Orange and the White,
> Good luck to dear old Texas Aggies,
> They are the boys that show the
> Real old fight . . ."

Someone pushed up beside her. Sammy turned to look into her twin's brown eyes. "Chuck!"

He warded down the arms she was about to throw around him. "Easy, Sam! Gosh, you look good!" The glow in his face died as he spoke to Don. "Howdy, Mr. Stuart, sir." Don flushed.

"You do not call an upperclassman 'sir' if either he or you is accompanied by a guest, Fish Forrester."

"Excuse me, sir—I mean, Mr. Stuart. I'm just trying to show the proper respect, sir."

Don's jaw hardened. After a minute he said quietly, "You're taking advantage of the situation. But I am still giving you permission to talk to your sister for twenty minutes after yell practice."

The cheer leaders had begun the swaying chant that called for linked arms. Sammy took the chance to hush her brother by extending a crooked elbow to either boy. In a minute lines of Aggie fans were rocking left, then right, in tune with the rhythmic chant:

> "Saw old Bevo's horns off,
> Saw old Bevo's ho-o-orns off——"

Bevo was the name of Texas University's mascot, a calf. Sammy addressed a silent, fervent appeal to her twin to use some discretion. As soon as the rally was over, most of the students flowed toward the Memorial Student Center and the dance. Don caught Sammy's hand.

"I'll wait for you in the lobby of the MSC. I think you'd rather have a chance to talk in private. Forrester, you'll escort your sister to the lobby?"

"I certainly will, Mr. Stuart. After all, I have a mild interest in her welfare."

Don's eyes narrowed and he spun away into the crowd.

"Well!" said Sammy, facing Chuck. "You really try, don't you?"

CHAPTER NINE

Chuck grunted. "If I have to call 'em 'sir,' I don't see why I shouldn't do it in front of visitors. Might as well let everybody see how democratic we are."

"Oh Chuck, you're in the Corps and you knew from the start it runs on military lines! Now what's been going on? Your letters haven't been models of information."

"I'm posting a one-point-nine index."

"Almost a B? Well, that's better than you did in high school. What *is* eating you?"

He cast her a suspicious look. "Didn't Stuart tell you? I got a Court and I'm not going home with you after the game. I'm restricted to this crummy campus till mid-December."

Wanting to show her sympathy and still talk some reason

into his fiery red head, Sammy put her hand through his arm. "Tell me what happened."

"Ragan was inspecting my room. Ran his white gloves over the windowsill, got a speck of dust. So he blessed me out and then he asked me all those Aggie 'Famous Facts'— how many conference championships has A & M won, what was the football team's most perfect record, the names of the deans and officials—all that stuff. He finally got me on the names of the living Aggies with the Congressional Medal of Honor. Should have heard him! When I had all I could take, I told him to get out."

"Before you threw him out?"

Chuck laughed glumly. "That was the general idea."

"You just can't let him foul you up," Sammy chided. "Are you going to let someone like that keep you in hot water when you've wanted to be an Aggie ever since you could reach up and pat Dad's boots?"

"Kid, this is a great school to be from, but it's not so good to be *at*. Morning formation, march to meals, march here, march there, sit on the front half of your chair in the mess hall and get served last, answer cush questions———"

"*What* kind of questions?"

"Oh, before you get cush—that's dessert—the upper-classmen ask questions. It's not all Ragan, Sam. I'm sick of the whole works."

She tugged at his arm. "All freshmen get the same deal, Chuck. Uncle Voss, Dad, Whit . . ."

"Whit!" Chuck kicked savagely at a pebble. "Sure, he eats it up. He's a wing commander, Distinguished Military Student, Ross Volunteer—he sits on Courts for guys like me! I don't blame him for that, he didn't have much option. I violated the darned Articles, and I'd do it again." Chuck stopped walking, and gazed mournfully at the Prexy's Moon, the light on the dome of the Academic Building. "I'm a maverick, Sam. I plain don't like this chain of command with me as the bottom link."

"Have you polished Dad's boots lately?"

Pulling free, Chuck quickened his pace. "Don't lecture me about switching plans! You and Whit sure did a hun-dred-and-eighty-degree turn."

"I didn't count on his making the Air Force a career, silly!"

"And I, madame, didn't know that I'd have to bow down to these two-bit tyrants morning, noon, and night."

"Okay, kettle, the pot will keep quiet and let you bubble on. But what do you have in mind? Staying restricted the rest of your A & M career, wearing a rut in the Bull Ring while you walk off demerits, or what?"

"I have a high motive. I mean to get Ragan out of the Corps. I've read up on the Articles, lady, and you let him break one around me! I'll turn him in so fast he won't know what hit him."

"Is that straight shootin', Hickok?"

"As straight as the way he's done me."

Sammy let it drop. She knew the only reason a lot of boys lasted the fish year was the bright hope of when they'd be upperclassmen and wield power. If thoughts of vengeance would keep Chuck in school, then let him have them. He took her inside the MSC and left her with Don.

It was an informal dance, with most of the couples coming straight from the drill field. As Sammy followed Don through the fox trot the combo was playing, she caught herself watching for Whit's curly brown head, checking the owner of each pair of senior boots. Don's voice interrupted the search.

"Are you mad at me because of Chuck?"

She glanced up. "Oh golly, no! You were forbearing as could be at yell practice, and I know Chuck can be a mule —it's one of our shared characteristics." She swallowed, thinking of her twin. "I—I'm sorry, though, that he's having a bad time."

"All fish do." Don changed the subject, his gray eyes lighting up with pride. "I'm glad you could come, Sammy. That's a gorgeous dress. Not fussy, but the style and that material really set you off."

"Thanks," Sammy smiled, and then, suddenly, her feet turned to wood though, mechanically, they kept time with Don's.

Whit was dancing in the corner. With a blonde who was a downright catastrophe in clinging white wool jersey with gold clips. Pale hair caught back in a Grecian knot, flawless ivory skin, she was too perfect to be endured, a striking contrast to Whit's dark, angular attractiveness.

As soon as the number ended, Sammy made for the powder room. Whit's date was a woman, not a girl! She had more poise and assurance than any ten of the other girls combined.

It wasn't fair! Woefully, Sammy examined herself in the mirror. She looked like what she was, all right. An eighteen-year-old from the brushland got up in a pretty, well-mannered gown that suited her and was quite handsome. But not devastating, not maddening, like that supple white jersey. Several girls came in on a burst of laughter and sent inquiring looks at Sammy.

She began to comb her hair, standing at the plate-glass mirror till she was able to smile and walk out. The dance was well under way now. She couldn't brood, for the constant tap-tap of boys cutting in kept her busy making small talk to new partners.

The dance went on and on. Sammy drank orange pop till she was sure she'd hate it forever, talked with feverish gaiety to Don and her other dancing acquaintances. In spite of all she could do, her gaze kept threading back to Whit and the blonde head lifted so attentively to him.

It hadn't taken him long. And what a beauty! Sammy felt as if a slim blade had made a subtle wound in her heart which opened each time she breathed. During her talk with Mrs. Halley she had decided that if Whit made overtures, she'd meet him halfway . . . What a dope she'd been! He hadn't been exactly locking himself up with his lessons. *I've gone with Lee, of course, but that's different.*

The combo moved into "Stardust," the song Sammy teamed in her heart with Whit, and her blood pulsed weepingly along with the music. *"Sometimes I wonder why I spend the lonely nights . . ."*

Eyes fixed beyond her partner's shoulder, Sammy didn't see Whit till his voice made her start. "May I?" he asked the boy she was with, and then she was fitting into his arms, matching his steps, as if nothing had ever happened. But though their bodies remembered, the direction of their hopes still separated them.

"How've you been?" he asked after a long moment.

"Fine. It seems you have too."

"Hmmm?"

"The girl. The blonde. She's beautiful."

Whit nodded, glancing toward his date who was circling the floor with another senior. "Should be. She's studying fashion and design at Baylor. Models in her spare time."

Ouch! Talk about competition. "How interesting." Sammy murmured, trying not to sound as jealous as she felt.

"Did you come up to see Chuck?" Whit questioned.

"Partly." So Whit thought she was stranded without him, did he? "I'm Don Stuart's date. Which is fortunate, since, as you know, Chuck is restricted to the campus."

A muscle corded in Whit's lean cheek. He ignored her last thrust. His hand pressed in hard on the small of her back, and his tone sounded harsh.

"Well, I-I'm glad you're dating, Sam. It's the best thing for us both to do."

"Of course it is." Sammy tried to sound gay and reasonable though a deep hurt twisted in her heart. "Lee thought it would be nice for me to come up."

"Lee? Who's that?"

"Oh," Sammy said as if making a discovery, "that's right, you don't know him. He's an oil man. Nice."

"How old is he?"

"Twenty-six."

Whit missed a beat, the first time in Sammy's memory. When he spoke, she was sure he had rejected several blunter reactions. "What does your Uncle Voss think about it—your going with someone that much older?"

"Uncle Voss likes Lee tremendously. He's given him a lease on our east pasture, in fact."

"That so?"

"Yes, that's so."

They danced in silence till the dance ended, further apart than they had even been during the past months. If you love me say so! Sammy thought despairingly. Oh, Whit, let's decide what we're going to do, please . . .

But he merely thanked her gravely when the music stopped, walked her to the edge of the dance floor, and waited till Don caught up with them. The boys spoke and Whit moved away.

"I brought you," Don said, waving off the converging stag line. "There's only one dance left and I want it!"

"Fine!" Sammy laughed and went into his arms with a brilliant smile. Whit was evidently doing his best to forget her. She'd try too.

She tried so spiritedly that Don, driving her to Halley's, asked if he could come down from San Antonio during the

Christmas holidays and see her. She glanced at him in dread.

Surely, oh surely, she hadn't involved another person in her troubles. She spoke with casual friendliness.

"Why, Chuck and I would love to have you come down. If you like horseback riding, we can keep you entertained and you'd enjoy Uncle Voss."

Don stretched his arm along the back of the seat as he parked in front of Halley's. "It wasn't a family outing I had in mind," he said with wry amusement. "You have a steady back in the brush?"

"Sort of."

Nicely, so fast she couldn't object or be annoyed, Don kissed her. "All right. We had fun this evening and we'll have fun tomorrow. If that steady ever crumbles, let me know?"

"You bet I will," Sammy laughed.

He took her to the door, thanked her ceremoniously for the date, and said he would be by around noon.

After a quick meal the next afternoon, Don had to join the other seniors around the flagpole in front of the Academic Building for the Elephant Walk. Sammy watched, with other dates and wives and parents, as the booted cadets wandered about like old elephants hunting a lonely spot to die. It meant that this was the last ball game during which they'd be part of the famous Twelfth Man, the united Corps which backed the team.

There was Whit. He wore the three diamonds of a Cadet Colonel and the blue and gold insignia of the Air Force ROTC, a winged propeller. Sammy flinched, and looked directly at that girl from Baylor.

The blonde looked store-window-groomed and lovely even in the nipping wind that lowered Sammy's southern temperature in more ways than one. That honey-beige suit —didn't it have any decorum? Didn't it know that suit should look businesslike? Sammy gazed at the flagpole till Don joined her and they started for Kyle Field.

Cars were parked solid for blocks and the whole area was congested with people. They finally made their way to the section where the Corps was. Since all the cadets had to stand throughout the game, their girls stood too, and most wore low heels like Sammy.

The model, though, wore three-inch heels and a mink stole, with a corsage pinned to her beige suit. Sammy resolutely decided not to look in her direction even if a touchdown play was going on at that end.

Down by the TU goal, some chaps-wearing, cowboy-attired Texas University boys had brought in their cannon, and their mascot, Bevo, who didn't look much like the Longhorn he represented. The seats filled till the cadet section was a mass of khaki interspersed with girls' bright clothing.

The bands played, and the TU team, orange and white, ran onto the field. Then all the A & M seniors poured out of the stands, a long stream of booted young men, forming a double line which made an arch for the Aggie football team to run under.

In spite of her resolve, Sammy saw Whit climb back to his place beside the Baylor girl, and more than the wind stung her eyes. Looking hastily around, she located Chuck and waved to him. She had some talking to do with that young man.

"Breakfast in the morning?" she called to him through cupped hands. He nodded and punched out with his elbows at the jokingly envious cadets on either side of him.

Sammy hardly kept up with the game. She clapped and yelled when Don did, and groaned along with the Corps' agony. Her eyes *would* slip toward Mavis whatever-her-name-was.

Who was she? Did Whit like her a lot? Had he dated her even last year? She didn't look like the sort to live on a ranch. The Officers' Wives' Club would be more her speed. During the half, Sammy watched her go down the exit to the powder room.

A cream-smooth way of walking, slim ankles, seams straight. She was a prize package, all right. Plunged deep in gloomy comparisons, Sammy couldn't properly enjoy the 250-member Aggie marching band, though she usually felt that hearing it was worth the drive from Los Ladinos. Reveille, the Aggie mascot, ran with the band, barking spiritedly. The game was tied up, 7 to 7.

But after the half the Aggies had it. TU made two quick goals, and their cannon thundered each time. By the start of the last quarter some TU rooters were already chanting.

"Poor Aggies! Poor, poor Aggies!" Over and over. And

they kept it up, for the Aggies couldn't score again. The TU-A & M game was the most bitterly fought of the year, for they were arch-rivals.

As the game ended, one TU student, probably thinking he was followed by compatriots, made for the Aggie goalposts and started working them down. Chuck had made his way to Sammy, but at the sight of the TU boys, he roared and went tearing across the field. Other Aggies were right behind him, baying like bloodhounds.

The TU student skinned up the post and stood on the crossbar, fidgeting like a nervous cat while senior sabers waved at him and cadet arms tried to yank him down. Thanks to the police, who escorted him away, the TU fan wasn't hurt.

Chuck, glaring, came back to Sammy. "They beat us," he growled. "But those cotton-pickin' tea-sips can leave our goalposts alone!"

Our goalposts? He couldn't hate A & M quite as he pretended and defend it so quickly. Sammy hugged him but she had enough sense not to point out his inconsistency.

She had dinner with Don before he left for the holidays at home, and they parted on pleasant terms. Then, though it was only nine, Sammy went to Halley's and bed. The past two days had worn her out. She met Chuck at the MSC for breakfast.

"A lot of people stayed over last night," she said as they queued up in the cafeteria. "Looks as if everybody in Texas is eating here today."

"No," corrected Chuck. "Just the condemned and their relatives." But he managed a wry grin and Sammy drew comfort from the instinctive way he'd rushed to the school's defense last evening.

College was always a jar, particularly if it was a military one. By Christmas he'd be used to things and feel much better. His talk through the meal turned on Ragan and how he was going to catch him breaking some rule. On the assumption that any motive that kept Chuck in school had to be welcomed, Sammy kept quiet till they were saying good-bye.

"If it gets too rough, get out the saddle soap and work on Dad's boots," she advised. "If you want to wear them in three years, you'll have to take everything Ragan can dish out and pretend you like it."

"Hah!" snorted Chuck. But his hand stayed on hers an extra second, sort of wistfully. "Write me, Sam, even when I don't answer real fast. Will you?"

"Haven't I been?" she teased and blew him a kiss. He was her twin; but in some ways she felt like his mother.

Lee's car was in the drive when she got home. "Have you struck oil?" she cried, running up the verandah, where he sat with Uncle Voss. Both men laughed. Lee offered her his chair.

"Anything but! Durn machinery keeps breaking down, we get gas rainbows but nothing else, and you've been gone. Lose any glass slippers in Aggieland?"

"Never a one." She met his look steadily. "There aren't any Prince Charmings there anyhow, just Aggies with spurs and boots." *And Air Force insignia. And blondes.*

She told about the game, and something of Chuck's trouble. Uncle Voss had been counting on the holiday, for he loved Chuck like the son he'd never had, but he philosophically tamped his pipe.

"I got campused my first Thanksgiving too," he said. "Also Easter. Of course that gave me a chance to walk off my demerits in the Bull Ring, so I really didn't give a hoot. Fran called last night, Sammy. She wants you to help her figure out a play."

Lee nodded. "Oh yes. She mentioned that when we went to the show." At Sammy's startled glance he explained negligently. "I was in town after supplies and met Fran, so we went to a Western. For miles we galloped, and Fran told me what the Mexican heroine shouted while the men fought."

Even Lee! Sammy sternly told herself she had no right to feel betrayed. She talked a little longer, till Lee said he had to go but that he'd carry in her suitcase first. He caught up with her at her door where she had paused to silently greet San Isidro and thank him for staying the same.

"Was I right about the golden dress?" he asked, putting the bag inside her door.

"You were right about it being my best style," she said, ruefully thinking of the Baylor blonde. "I guess it's all a question of what a man likes."

"I know what I like," he said. He held her so intently with his gaze that the moment rose and beat between them.

With a genuine physical effort she moved back. "Good-by, Lee. Thanks for checking me in. I hope that oil comes in soon."

"That makes two of us." There was a grim twist to his mouth. "Sam. Now you've seen Whit, how do you feel?"

"I—I don't know." Sammy turned, blinking back tears. "Lee, he was with another girl."

Lee's hands caught her. "Good! I'm glad he was and I'm selfish enough to be glad you're back with me." His fingers brought up her face and he kissed her, hard. "Listen. I want you to think about me. Not that cadet."

Pleadingly, half frightened, she put her palms against his chest. "I'm mixed up. Please, I—I don't know what will happen."

"That's a good sign," he said in satisfaction. His hand brushed her cheek, and he was gone.

Sammy stared at San Isidro as if he might solve her problems. Her fingers strayed to her lips. Angrily she jerked them away. The best thing for her was to stop trying to figure out her tangled emotions. There was the English school. The coyote dun roving the little hills and, more immediately, Fran's play. Till she could remember with detachment she wouldn't think at all of Whit dancing with his head bowed to another girl's; or let herself feel again the warm strength of Lee's arms. It was impossible, wasn't it, to love two men? Especially if one loved a ranch too.

CHAPTER TEN

Sammy drove to Fran's boardinghouse Sunday after church to talk over the play, which Uncle Voss had vaguely explained as some kind of Christmas program. Fran greeted her with such exuberance that, in spite of a stab of jealousy, Sammy had to laugh.

"You must have enjoyed that movie!"

Fran's grin had a trace of guilt but she looked Sammy squarely in the eye. "Well, let's say the company, if not the show, was full-screen and three-dimension." She pushed back her auburn hair. "I like that man!"

Strange. Fran was pretty and as old as that blonde model, but there was nothing formidable about her, she didn't have that tantalizing perfection and seductive stance. You're either born with it or not, Sammy decided. Not that I'd like looking Mavis' way as a steady thing, but once in awhile, it's come in handy. Say when you're trying to get your boy friend back.

". . . about the play."

Fran's upraised voice shook Sammy from her resentful musings. She turned. "Oh. Yes. The program. Well, do you have anything to start with?"

"Twenty-seven assorted kids."

"Mmm." Sammy rubbed her forehead. "The parents are going to watch?"

"Yes, each class is giving an entertainment for the pupils' families."

"Won't there be a big overlap? Some families will have a child in almost every grade."

"That's true, and I brought it up at teachers' meeting." Fran grimaced. "No one else thought it mattered. They said not many parents come anyway, and it would be too hard to stage an all-school program that would appeal to both Anglo and Latin families."

Sammy pondered. "It still seems that the parents would be more apt to come to a program where they could see all their children instead of having to skip some of their individual class plays."

"The staff already thinks I talk too much for the junior-junior faculty member, but I'd bring it up again, provided we had a really good suggestion."

"Let's see. Whatever it is, it needs to interest both Latins and Anglos, needs to have a lot of parts and yet not take too long. There are six grades. About how many children are enrolled?"

"Right at one hundred and fifty." At Sammy's distressed whistle, Fran added, "They needn't all have speaking parts. Songs and dances could absorb the majority. Got any ideas, however desperate?"

Thinking aloud, Sammy racked her brain. "Once at San Jose Mission in San Antonio we saw *Los Pastores*— it's wonderful. But it's terribly long and the speaking parts would be rough for children. Besides, it's in Spanish so that Anglos wouldn't understand." She held her chin in her hands a few minutes, thinking back, then straightened with a whistle of delight.

"*Las Posadas!*"

"What—or which—is that?" demanded Fran.

"It means *The Inns* and is sort of a play about how Joseph and Mary tried to find shelter and finally went to the manger. It's much easier to put on than *Los Pastores,* and less expensive, so it's often performed along the Rio at Christmas."

"It doesn't sound as if it'd have many speaking parts. Besides, isn't it in Spanish too?"

"As uncomplicated as it is, told mostly through actions, I think we could get around the language barrier. Besides, we could just use the basic idea and work in some other parts. The Latins know the dialogue at the inns by heart, so that could be put into English. And we could make the narrative into a sort of choral reading, alternating English and Spanish so as not to lose the flow or sense of the story. I bet we could talk to Miss Turner, the English and Speech teacher, and she'd give us some pointers on technique."

Fran still had a wrinkle between her carefully plucked eyebrows, but she nodded. "I like what you say, if it can be worked out. Let's see if Miss Turner can spare us some time."

The high school teacher, whom Sammy remembered with affection, was glad to talk with them. By the end of the short walk to her home, Sammy had come up with some frills which she explained enthusiastically as they sat at the big table Miss Turner used for a desk.

"Maybe we could get off to a good start by having a child putting out his stocking and thinking of Santa Claus, then switch to a Mexican child putting his shoe in the window for the Three Wise Men to fill. You know, they ride by on camels and leave gifts. This would lead naturally to why the Wise Men came, and *Las Posadas,* don't you think?"

"I can't, at this point," Fran sighed. "Let's go back over it slowly. *Muy, muy despacio.*"

They did, for two hours, while Miss Turner jotted down notes and suggestions. She looked over her glasses and her face was flushed with pleasure, so that she looked breath-less and youthful, almost pretty.

"This can be very effective, girls. Of course it'll need imaginative work and considerable care because you'll be combining two languages and splicing extras onto a tradi-tional play. The choral reading group can narrate the opening tableaux of Santa and the Wise Men." She tapped her pencil. "The group needs more than that to do, else they'll fidget."

Fran had taken fire over the plan and now she leaned forward. "Why not have them chant some kind of refrain after Mary and Joseph are turned away from each inn? And perhaps we could work out other places for them to speak."

"That's a good idea!" Miss Turner put down her pencil with a satisfied air.

"I'm so happy you let me help brainstorm on this, girls. Instead of hogging the holy day for Santa and our modes of celebrating, this shares the Mexican tradition. It should fascinate everybody."

Fran picked up the notes, smiling. "I'm glad to hear you say that. Because I'm going to tackle the principal and the rest of the staff about it in the morning."

"I'll tell Mr. Alden what I think about it," Miss Turner promised. "Also, I'll help with rehearsal in my spare periods." She brandished a fragile hand in a most un-dignified fashion. "You put it to Mr. Alden, and I'll follow up! Let me know any time you need help."

"Thanks," they chorused, and walked out into the crisp, bright weather.

"We can practice at English school too," Sammy said. "Oh, this ought to be fun!"

"Yes, if I can just talk Mr. Alden into it. I don't think the other teachers will mind as long as it won't make them extra work." Fran suddenly stopped dead. "Wait a minute! Who's going to make up the parts for the choral group?" She in-stantly poked a finger into Sammy's ribs. "You can!"

Blinking, Sammy protested, "Hold on! I can't——"

"Why not? You know *Las Posadas* and you're a bilingual. Those rhymes and chants you've made up for the English school prove you have a knack for that sort of thing. Try it, Sammy, please!"

"I'll try," Sammy promised gingerly after mulling it over. After sparking the project she could hardly leave all the work up to others. "You can tell me tomorrow if Mr. Alden okays it."

"You bet I will."

Driving home, Sammy reflected that Fran was certainly kept busy. Teaching didn't end with classwork and grading papers. To give your help, your skill, your understanding—that could serve as a focus for life. There wouldn't be much time left to feel sorry for yourself, brood over old problems. Whit's gray eyes seemed to watch her quizzically; biting her lip, she thrust him back under the safe heading of "Old Problems," just as she filed Lee under "Future Difficulties."

How would it be to teach, as a full-time job? For the first time Sammy tried to visualize what would happen if Whit and she couldn't work out their plans. She realized now, with a sense of loss for a time gone forever, that horses and the ranch weren't enough. She needed someone to love, she wanted to be loved. This golden, thorny world was not able in itself to fill her life. At present she had the English school and Lee's company, the dream of the elusive coyote dun up in the hills, but these wouldn't last. What would she do?

Follow Whit into the Air Force? She shrank at the thought. It was doubtful she would even be asked, what with blonde Mavis on the scene. Moodily Sammy got out to open the gate. Sometimes she was glad it was a long time till spring and the time of decision.

She worked that night on the narrative parts. For the child hanging up a stocking for Santa, the chorus could say part of "The Night Before Christmas." Then they could chant the pantomimed thoughts of the little Mexican boy as he placed his shoe in the window:

> "In the night come the Three Kings,
> Balthaser, Gasper, Melchoir.
> They brought good gifts to the Sweet Lord.
> Now in my shoe they'll leave presents."

Through that transition to the wanderings of the Holy Family. At each inn Joseph would ask for shelter and be refused; then the light voices in the reading group could say:

"Poor Mary!
Poor Joseph!
Poor *Niño Santo*!
No lodging in the inn,
No room in hearts of men.
On, on they wander."

Then the dark voices would announce:

"Look!
A light!
They knock now."

Sammy worked till midnight, taking a new kind of pleasure in seeing her ideas take on real shape and form. Wouldn't it be fun to hear it performed—something that wouldn't have been done if she hadn't worked at it?

After Fran took the town children home the next evening from Los Ladinos, she came back to see the narrative and have dinner. She read the script and laughed with a sincere delight that gave Sammy her first relaxed breath since her friend had asked to see the work.

"This is *good*, Sammy."

Pleased, Sammy explained. "I changed each innkeeper's excuse to give it more interest and reality."

"That is better than having them all give the same alibi," Fran approved. "I can hardly wait to show this to Mr. Alden!"

"What did he say?"

"Not much. He said he'd have to see a script and think it over, though he did like the possibility of drawing in a large audience and having one impressive program instead of six small ones. You can't blame him for being cautious. This is unusual enough to attract notice, and it could bring either credit or ridicule on him and the school."

With Uncle Voss an amused but interested listener, they talked on about the play, and after the meal, while the girls were doing dishes, Fran said again that teaching along the Border was much different from teaching in a homogeneous community—harder but more fun.

"Why did you apply down here?" Sammy asked.

Fran laughed drily. "I wanted to get a long way from Beaumont, and this seemed to fill the bill."

"What's wrong with Beaumont?"

"I could say I wanted a change from the town I'd always lived in, but I could have stayed happily in Beaumont forever—if the lad I was engaged to hadn't met and married a gorgeous half-Cherokee gal up in Oklahoma and brought her back to dwell in ye olde home town." Fran shuddered. "My friends were feeling sorry for me—watching and testing me the way a thermometer tests roasting beef. When I was well cooked, overdone in fact, I applied for the most distant vacancy I could find."

Uncomfortably avoiding Fran's eyes, Sammy polished a glass. "I—I'm sorry. I shouldn't have been so nosy."

Fran gave a wave of her arm. "Think nothing of it. I'd rather he fell for another girl *before* instead of *after* we were married. Besides, I think he and I were simply used to each other. High school steadies, all that. We made a team, our friends and families looked at us as a pair, and there was no reason to break off anything so companionable. . . . Till Jack found out about love." Fran scrubbed harder than necessary at the table. "Now I really don't know how much of my feeling was heartbreak and how much wounded pride. I don't think I loved him deeply, because I'm pretty well recovered."

Was she saying in a veiled way that she could get interested seriously in Lee? Sammy quickly dodged the question. Lee had dated Fran once and he could certainly do it again; Fran was free to attract him.

Rather abruptly Sammy said, "I'm anxious to hear what Mr. Alden thinks of the play. You'll show it to him tomorrow?"

"I'll be waiting at his office when he comes in," Fran said with an emphatic nod and then she was off.

Mr. Alden approved the *Las Posadas* program and practice started on it immediately. Several times a week Sammy used part of English school to teach the choral refrains. Except for Rudi, who had the part of the child setting out his shoes for the Three Kings, all the others would be in the reading group.

Lee was still putting in formidable hours, but he stopped by once or twice a week and a few times they went out to dinner and a show. Sammy got him to stay at the ranch and talk when she could, in preference to driving to town, for he had grown thin and his eyes were bruised-looking.

She rode by once in awhile, not taking Lee from his work but just looking. The crew slept in town, but Doodlebug fed them; since five men had to be at the rig all the time, there was a constant parade of changing shifts, being the cook was no small chore. The fireman of each shift made coffee and washed the crew's overalls in a fifty-gallon oil drum hooked up to steam and water.

A series of mishaps had plagued the Sammy-*Mula* Number One. In addition to the alcoholic tool-pusher, the drilling equipment was temperamental.

"Been going through gas sand for a hundred and thirty feet," Doodlebug told Sammy one day in mid-December when she stepped into his mess hall for coffee. "Just to finish the grief, the drill pipe twisted off close to the bottom of the hole this morning and they're fishin' for it."

"Fishing?"

"You bet. They've put down a larger pipe, tapered to slip over the twisted-off section and raise it up. But they're down over two thousand feet, so you can imagine what a job that'll be."

Sammy took a long gulp of coffee. "I don't see how Lee can miss ulcers and an early death in this business! Always something."

"That's life," scorned Doodlebug, gazing wistfully down at the laboring men on the derrick. "I still say this is the wrong place. He needs to be on the other side of this formation. That's where my peach twig pulls down."

This was no time to bother Lee, who was directing the recovery job. Sammy rode home, looping about by the little hills.

Where was the coyote dun? Was he going to haunt her but never be caught, as Loney obsessed Uncle Voss? Now in the winter, when there weren't any watermelons to fool with or much less to do, Martín and the *vaqueros* ought to track the wild horse down. If they didn't do something toward his capture by New Year's, she'd nudge Martín a bit. Right now, though, there was so much to do.

She and Fran took one Saturday to go shopping in San Antonio. For Lupe a cashmere shawl and earrings, for Martín a new hat, for each person on the ranch some gift. Doodlebug got a red wool shirt, Uncle Voss a silver-gray Stetson. A broad silver and onyx bracelet seemed the thing for Fran, and of course Chuck should have records and a casual pullover.

Thank goodness, Chuck would have to answer her questions when she confronted him in person. His letters ignored her efforts to learn how he was getting along with Ragan and A & M generally. He wrote seldom and then only about classes and externals. He never mentioned Whit either, and Sammy tried to tell herself that she was glad.

"I hope Chuck isn't taking his discipline the hard way," Uncle Voss said worriedly after one of the noncommittal letters. "He has lots of fire. If he gets off on the wrong foot, he could be as poor an officer as he could be a fine one."

"Oh, if he gets through this first semester he ought to have it made," Sammy encouraged. "Chuck may care more about the school than he realizes. I told you how he jumped out to defend the goalposts at the Texas game."

Anyhow, he'd soon be home, and then they'd know how he was getting along. Lupe was practicing already on his favorite foods and talking happily about her Chuck whose picture, in cadet uniform, she kept in the kitchen, a safe distance above the sink.

It took Sammy a long time to locate a gift for Lee. Finally, in the jewelers where Fran got a signet ring for her father, Sammy found a pair of derrick-shaped cuff links in gold, with a tie clasp to match. She had them specially wrapped, pleased at such an appropriate find. Of course, now, he'd better bring in oil or these would be a reminder of the operation that broke him.

The last stop in San Antonio was the most fun—to choose a *piñata* and its stuffing of candy, gum, and trinkets, for the Christmas party Sammy was giving the children from the English school. From the dozens of large papier-mâché figures, Sammy picked a blue reindeer with gold-foil antlers. Its yard-long body was hollow inside. After it was filled with the treats, it would be hung from the ceiling and the children, blindfolded, would try to hit and break it with sticks.

On the Friday before Christmas vacation Sammy got things ready. Uncle Voss put up a pulley for the stuffed reindeer and padded a broom handle for a striking implement. Lupe had made the huge thermos jug full of hot chocolate and there were marshmallows to float in the cups. Lee had promised to stop by if he possibly could. Martín had fetched in a small salt cedar from the hills and planted it in a tub.

Sammy had assembled all the Christmas ornaments she could dig up, and when the children came, the first part of the fun was decorating the tree.

When the children had strung on every available light and ball and icicle, Juana was allowed to plug in the electric cord.

"Ooohh!" came the delighted chorus of indrawn breaths. Some whispered, *"Lindísima!"* but there was a goodly share of "Beautiful!"

The star of Bethlehem may have perched a bit awry on the slender peak, and the hypercritical might have sniffed that you could scarcely see the tree for the trimming, but Sammy, through a mist, thought it was the most lovely tree she'd seen since she grew up.

Games followed the trimming, and then songs, both Spanish and English. Fran had a good voice, and Tomás, present for the festivities, helped lead, his black eyes alternately dancing and solemn as the mood of the carols changed, from "God Rest Ye Merry Gentlemen" to the haunting Spanish "Cradle Song of the Madonna."

> Then, you who walk among the palms,
> Holy angels,
> Because my baby is sleeping,
> Hold the branches!

While they were singing "Joy to the World," Sammy heard a light tap on the door. Opening, she looked into Diego Ruiz's hawklike eyes. He held out a willow basket covered with a spotless cloth.

"My wife made little sweet cakes for the party, Señorita Sam. Carlos told us it would be today." He looked down at his boot, swallowed, and almost glared at her. "I have the wish to thank you for teaching him. He does well in school, he is happy. I suppose it is best that he forget the old ones, our old town."

"He doesn't have to forget, Diego. Come to the school play tonight and see. Now come in and help celebrate. We'll soon be through."

"Well—" Diego glanced in; his gaze softened as it fell on Carlos' excited face. "I might. In order to take my son home."

Diego was barely settled when Lee arrived, with soft balls

for the boys and jumping ropes for the girls. He joined the onlookers, and after another song the *piñata* was lowered from the pulley. Tomás gleefully manipulated the reindeer on its rope, jerking it high just in time to save it from being hit, as each child took his blindfolded turn at swatting it. Juana landed a mighty thwack on one leg, and Chuey hit the nose but it survived the contest, so the blindfold was discarded and the third assailant broke through the blue crepe-paper body, spilling candy, bubble gum, balloons, whistles, toy watches, and rings all over. There was a mad scramble, skirts and blue jeans swishing under chairs and benches, into corners.

Two minutes later the last peppermint stick had been picked up, and fists and pockets bulged. Sammy and Fran poured chocolate and marshmallows into paper cups, and as each child collected his, he also took one of the sweet cakes Diego had brought.

"*Mamacita* made these cakes," Carlos announced proudly. "She made them because I learn well from Señorita Sam." And he reached up to bestow a chocolate-and-marshmallow kiss on her cheek.

Sammy hugged him. For his sake alone, she was glad for the English school.

Lee gave his presents to several of the children to pass out at the door as Fran herded them out to her car. After the last delighted youngster had gone, crying. "*Felices Pascuas!*" and "Merry Christmas!" Sammy turned to Lee.

"That was a party!" she laughed, picking up the reindeer's head and stroking it. "The kids loved the ropes and balls, Lee. It was nice of you to bring them."

"The fun was all mine!" He reached for the wastebasket and made himself useful as she began cleaning up the room. "They're such cute, well-behaved little sprouts. You handle 'em skillfully too. Which amuses me no end!"

"Why?" asked Sammy, straightening in defiance.

Lee grinned. "Because you seem so young to me. I wouldn't have the faintest notion of how to cope with this group, while you have them speaking English and singing and even kissing teacher. An excellent tradition, by way. One I wouldn't want to break."

Taking her shoulders in his hands, Lee kissed her. "If you insist, I'll get mistletoe to make it official," he said. "Tomorrow's Christmas Eve. Will you be home?"

"Yes." Sammy fought the impulse to touch her lips wonderingly. "Come if you can, please. My brother gets home tomorrow. I want you to meet him. Can you make the school program tonight?"

"I'm afraid not. We finally fished out that drill pipe but this gas sand is giving us trouble." He rubbed his eyes.

In a rush of worry Sammy caught his arm. "Did you get any sleep last night?"

The old teasing glint showed in his gaze. "Why sleep when I can think about you? So long, *Lindísima,* it was a lovely party!"

I hope he hits it, Sammy thought, watching him move toward the car with his long, leggy stride. I hope he gets a good well.

Shaken by the intensity of her feeling, she wondered in shock, *Could I be—starting to love him*? But Whit's face slipped over Lee's, hiding the green *onza* eyes, and Sammy knelt, blindly picking up the shattered pieces of the reindeer.

CHAPTER ELEVEN

At eight o'clock that night the school auditorium was jam-packed. Word had gotten around that *Las Posadas* was being featured, given a place of honor, and the people wanted to see it. Near the back sat Diego Ruiz with his wife and little girl, their eyes riveted on the swaying curtains, which would soon open and show them Carlos and the old, beloved tradition of Mexico.

Sammy sat with Lupe, Uncle Voss, and the other ranch people; Fran was in the wings. When the curtains drew back, the choral reading group, dressed in choir robes borrowed from all available churches, stood on tiered benches at the back of the stage, with space in front for the dramatic action.

The beginning pantomime of the children watching for Santa and the Three Kings led into the entry of the Holy Family. A real burro, his hoofs swathed in burlap, had been borrowed for the play, and a very small Mary sat precariously sideways upon him, hanging to Joseph's arm. Joseph, luckily, was a sixth-grader, and strong. He maneuvered the donkey, kept Mary aloft, and somehow managed to remember his lines as he accosted the first innkeeper:

> "Sir, I beg of you
> In all your charity
> To give shelter to this Lady."

At last, after each innkeeper turned away the wanderers, after the choral group had chanted each time their shocked and pitying refrain, the curtains fell, to reveal upon reopening the Baby in His straw bed with the patient little burro batting an ear above Him while the parents gave thanks.

While Mr. Alden, Miss Turner, and the rest of the staff accepted the glowing thanks of the audience, Fran came down from the stage and gave Sammy a hug.

"A triumph worthy of Napoleon!" she exulted. "I'll leave for Beaumont in the morning feeling no pain. In fact, I think I'll wire ahead for them to have the ticker tape out!"

Parents swept Fran away. Sammy, watching the children bask in their families' compliments, was grateful she had had something to do with it. Especially when Mrs. Ruiz shyly came over and greeted her in the English she hadn't known seven weeks before.

"Señorita Sam, it was beautiful." She lapsed into Spanish. "I am happy it was *Las Posadas* and so is my Diego. He says perhaps we can remember the good things of our past and still live gladly now. Things like this play—they help our children to be proud of the old things instead of despising them." She pressed a tiny object into Sammy's hand. "A medal of Our Lady of Guadalupe. Please keep it." She smiled and fled after her husband.

Sammy looked down at the dark Madonna, Mexico's patroness. When Cortes conquered Mexico, he brought, along with his horses, the taste and sound of Spain—the knight's saddle and spurs, the mantilla, the cross and rosary. Spain's customs had spread a graceful, if often cruel, veneer over the centuries-old Indian ways. Some of the old gods had taken refuge disguised as saints, the carved stone serpent might peer from under an altar, and it was rumored that even Guadalupana was closely related to a beneficent rain goddess.

Smiling, Sammy put the little medal in her handkerchief.

Next morning she drove to San Antonio to meet Chuck. He got off the bus with two suitcases and collected three boxes from the storage beneath the coach.

"Good grief!" Sammy marveled. "You brought home everything you own, it looks like!"

"I just about did. Want me to drive?"

"Have at it."

Once they were headed out of town, Sammy flicked a glance at her twin. He was wearing the regulation crew cut at its maximum length, a finger's width, and his bony frame had filled out. He looked tailored and military but not exactly joyous. She attempted humor.

"How's the old school, you fightin' Texas Aggie?"

"When you call me that, smile," he said—only he didn't. "How's Uncle Voss? Is Lupe okay?"

Sammy briefed him on the state of things at Los Ladinos. "Lee's coming for presents tonight so you'll get to know him," she ended.

"That the oil man?" Chuck sounded unusually interested. A warning "twin twinge" in Sammy's ribs made her eye her brother suspiciously.

"Of course Lee's the oil man. How many men do you think I've been dating? Anyhow, why do you care?"

Chuck scowled. "Because I'd like to talk about the business, dear sister." He switched the subject. "Don asked me yesterday if you were still going steady. You made a hit with him, Sam."

"He's nice, but he'll have to find another girl. When are you going to get one, pal?"

"A fish whose second home is the Bull Ring has no time for distractions," Chuck said dourly. He sounded as if he were quoting someone.

Why didn't he tell her how Whit was? The question almost popped out several times, but she fought it back. Let anyone, even her twin, see that she was still waving a torch? Not if she bit her tongue out!

Chuck fidgeted as they neared the ranch, frequently half turning to her. Sammy, avenging herself for his failure to report on Whit, didn't help him, but hummed a tune and surveyed the country.

"Sam," he burst out, as they stopped by the iron gate, "keep Uncle Voss off me about school, will you? I want to forget the darn place awhile."

Troubled by the desperation in his tone, Sammy promised, "I'll try." She wanted to ask some questions herself, but Chuck's manner forbade it. Later, when he felt like it, he'd talk.

Most of the ranch people were on hand when they drove up to the front of the house. Uncle Voss came down the veranda in two strides, gripping Chuck by the shoulders, then out-and-out hugging him. "It's good to have you back, son! You keeping those boots polished?"

Chuck muttered something and it seemed to Sammy that his face contorted as he turned to kiss Lupe and shake the hands of Martín and the *vaqueros,* tousle the heads of the staring children.

As soon as Lee came that night, they celebrated Christmas Eve. This was the one time of year that Sammy missed the North with its snow and nippy weather.

With palm trees and bougainvillaea flashing beside the crimson hibiscus, it didn't seem really like Christmas; still, this climate resembled that of Judea and Bethlehem. The Mexican story of camels and shoes was more appropriate than Santa and chimneys, so Sammy had made big silhouette camels against the wall behind the tree, and placed shoes in the window. On the buffet was the *créche,* lit by four candles, and the table held Lupe's praline and nougat, nuts, carmelized apples, on sticks, buttered popcorn, and a huge blue-and-white German bowl filled with spiced Mexican chocolate to be served in matching mugs.

The baskets holding presents for the ranch families were on the veranda. After the children were asleep, Uncle Voss and the twins would take the things by.

Lee and Chuck shook hands upon meeting and seemed to like each other at once. Now, as they sang carols, Sammy, sitting next to her twin, watched his face, ruddy and sensitive and determined in the firelight. How good it was to have him home!

Uncle Voss was evidently thinking the same thing, for he kept glancing at Chuck, and the smoke came from his pipe in placid, contented puffs. After they sang all the songs they could think of, including all the verses of "The Twelve Days of Christmas," they opened gifts. Chuck turned on the phonograph and played his new records on the spot,

Uncle Voss modeled his Stetson, and Lee changed cuff links, trying out the gold derricks.

"Hope they're a good omen," he said.

Sammy laughed up at him. "So do I!"

Surrounded by her booty, a white suede jacket from Uncle Voss, poetry from Chuck, a Michoacán *rebozo,* Sammy opened a packet that jangled enticingly. It was from Lee and she felt his eyes warm on her as she undid the rustling folds of white tissue.

Gold bangles, five of them! Each different, two plain, three etched with patterns. Sammy slipped them on, held up her arm, and listened to their gay music.

"Oh lovely!" she cried.

" 'Five golden rings . . .' " Lee smiled. "But I couldn't find the three French hens or the partridge in the pear tree."

It was late enough to deliver the gifts, so they all got in the station wagon and took the baskets to the homes of Jorge, Vicente, and Martín. At each house they were gifted back with hand-carved leather belts, woven mats and embroidery, expertly plaited rawhide ropes. At Martín's house, full of visiting relatives with whom Lupe was talking up a storm, Sammy received a promise.

"Señorita Sam," Martín said with dignity, his iron-gray hair shining in the light, "we have watched for the coyote dun, but he eludes us. It is time to go after him in a serious manner. As soon as the New Year comes, Jorge, Vicente, and I are going into the hills after the fashion of mustangers, and once we find his trail, we will pace him down and bring him to you." He bowed toward Uncle Voss. "That is, if you approve, *patrón.*"

Sammy met her uncle's gaze steadily as he asked, "Do you want him, Sammy? Do you want them to catch him?"

Why should she suddenly see Whit's dark head lifted to the flash of wings? She threw back her shoulders, making her hands into fists.

"Yes! I want him! The sooner the better."

"You reckon he'll take to a fenced pasture?"

"After awhile he will." With a touch of bitterness Sammy added, "We have to get used to things we don't like. Why shouldn't he?"

Turning, Uncle Voss nodded to Martín. "All right. But don't injure yourselves trying to get him."

Somehow, it left a bad taste in Sammy's mouth. She knew Uncle Voss hoped the dun would elude the men, and to make it worse, she had enough of the same feeling to taint her resolve to own him. Well, she thought sourly as they rode back to the house, Uncle Voss hunts Loney, who is free in the same way—so why should he blame me?

She felt even more let-down when Lee, after inviting Chuck and her over to see the well, said he had to get right back to camp. The drill bit had gone down so far that if anything was going to happen, it should do so pretty soon.

After Lee's departure Chuck lapsed into moody silence. When he didn't fend off her good-night kiss, Sammy knew he was far gone in some kind of trouble, but after a few questions she gave up. He'd talk when he was ready. Sufficient to the morrow was the evil thereof.

The day after Christmas she and Chuck mounted their horses and rode over to Tigre Creek. It was bitter cold, a blue norther having whipped in overnight, and after watching the work at the rig for a while, Sammy went up to the shelter of Doodlebug's cookhouse and his pungently steaming coffee. Lee joined her in a cup before he went back to the well. He looked as if he needed sleep rather than stimulants.

"He's wearin' himself to a nub," Doodlebug lamented with a shake of his white head. "If only he'd drilled when the twig pulled down—I *felt* it, Miss Sam—I felt the blamed oil!"

Sammy looked after Lee's khaki-clad figure. No matter how hard he worked, either the oil was there or it wasn't. She hoped desperately that it would be; but even if this well failed, Lee wouldn't. He'd find another company to throw in with, and eventually he'd make the big strike.

That was the difference. A person had no control over what lay under the ground, but he had the option to try again, to start fresh. Of course he couldn't do it by hanging around the dry well and moaning.

And that, decided Sammy, lifting her chin, applied to love as well as business. She thanked Doodlebug for the coffee, pulled on her gloves and jacket, and halloed Chuck away from the derrick.

Collars turned up against the biting cold, they were halfway home when Chuck said something. The wind tore the sound from Sammy's ears.

"What?" she shouted.

"I'm quitting school!" Chuck yelled back at her. "I'm going to work for Lee as soon as I square it with Uncle Voss."

Sammy caught hold of her saddlehorn. "You—you're *what?*"

"I'm through at A & M."

"Oh no!"

Chuck snapped his fingers. "Oh yes!"

Choked with the dozen things she wanted to say, Sammy finally came up with what she knew was a weak rejoinder. "Charles Forrester, whatever are you talking about?"

"My new job, Samuela," mimicked Chuck.

"But—school!"

"The heck with school!" Chuck whirled on her. His lips were white and the young bones showed harshly in his face. "I've had it—that pack of junior-grade tyrants! Now don't preach, Sam! I'm through."

Checking an outburst, Sammy rode by her twin in silence, trying to think of at least a stalling measure. This would be a terrible blow to Uncle Voss. In as reasonable a tone as she could produce, she said, "This is pretty important, fella. Why don't you think it over a couple of days?"

"Why do you think I brought all my stuff home?" he demanded. "I've been thinking about quitting since the first day, and it's gotten worse, not better. The Cadet Court same as said I had no control over who visited my room, all that jazz in the mess hall about being served last, standing at parade rest before the prayer while upperclassmen sit—oh, it's just not for me, that's all!"

After a pause Sammy asked, "Did you bring Dad's boots home?"

"That's a dirty dig, Sam."

"Well, did you?"

"As a matter of fact, I couldn't. They're drying out. Which gave me the last bit of fuel I needed to blast right out of that place."

"I'm no good at riddles. Would you explain?"

"Ragan got the boots. Soaked 'em in a fine compound of salt and vinegar."

Sammy flinched. Her eyes filled with stinging tears. "Dad's boots? Oh Chuck! How could anyone do that?"

A muscle twitched in Chuck's jaw. "I don't know, but he did. He brought them back and said it ought to teach me not to get my senior boots till I fit 'em."

"Didn't you report him?" Sammy blazed. "That's vandalism, that's housebreaking, that's——"

"Lousy." Chuck gave a barking laugh. "It's sort of funny. Those boots were the only thing that kept me in school after I got campused Thanksgiving, and a lot of times since. I kept telling myself that Dad and Uncle Voss went through the same thing and I couldn't let them down. But when Ragan threw them in my room—all curled and blistered, that did it. I socked him. We had quite a little party. He's plenty rough. But when my roommate yelled that Stuart was coming, Ragan shoved off. Guess he didn't want to explain the reason for our set-to."

"Did you tell Don what happened?"

"No. I'm not a cry-baby. Besides, I wanted to get Ragan for breaking the regs, not for a personal thing."

No wonder Chuck didn't want to go back. Just hearing about it twisted Sammy inwardly till she felt sick. "The boots—can we have them fixed? Oiled or something?"

"I doubt it, but I'll see, of course. The man who made them has a shop near the campus and I'll take them there when I go back to formally drop out."

"I can see why you're fed up. But there are other schools. Baylor, Rice, Texas U. Why don't you transfer?"

"I don't want to go to any of *them*."

Astonished at his note of disgust, Sammy stared at him. "Good grief, you don't like A & M, you can't stand the Corps, you've been wanting out since the day you registered! Another college should look good to you."

"It wouldn't seem like school. Gee, Sam, you ought to see that. Forresters always go to A & M. If I can't take it, I won't attend at all. Uncle Voss will feel better if I just say I'm not the higher-education type. He'd shrivel if I went to another place."

"Don't be stupid! You need an education. Don't throw it away even if you do have to give Uncle Voss some hard moments."

"I'd rather go to work. You knew that I wanted to go into oil after my hitch in the Air Force."

"Sure—as an engineer. Now you'll be a crewman. It won't matter now, but how about after you're married? Do you want to be moving your family around like a gypsy, and maybe not earn enough to send your kids to college?"

"Good Lord, who's got any kids?" Chuck howled. "Long before that day, sister dear, I intend to own my own company."

"Lee says it gets harder every day to make the grade as an independent. This is just cutting off your nose to spite your face. Won't you at least———"

Chuck blocked her way with his iron-gray gelding, and Chispa snorted and danced. "Look, Sam, when I tried to tell you about Whit and the Air Force, you cut me off. Now you've got to understand this is my decision. Okay?"

It wasn't, but what use to argue till she had some good ammunition? Detouring her brother, Sammy trotted Chispa toward the corral. One thing she could do—talk to Lee, persuade him not to hire Chuck. Maybe without a job Chuck would take a second look at things. What a mess to come up at Christmas! At least Chuck hadn't told Uncle Voss yet. She hoped he never would.

It got pretty bad after supper that evening while the Forresters all sat talking before the fire. Uncle Voss kept asking about A & M and reminiscing about his and Dad's Corps days.

"I'm so darn proud of you, Chuck," he said. "I never had a son, so you do double duty in our tribe. And when you're a senior you'll wear your father's boots."

Fidgeting, his knuckles white as he sat with his hands on his knees, Chuck gulped. "Sir, I———"

"Silver taps," Uncle Voss sighed, leaning back and filling his pipe, smiling as he dreamed back. "Aggie Muster—that's when Aggies got together wherever they are each year, and the roll call of those who have died during that year is called and taps are played. I remember the muster in Bataan, and your father mustered in France during the same war. . . . Some of the time you hate the school, but you never forget it after you leave, and you never forget your friends."

Chuck looked appealingly at Sammy. She hardened her heart and picked up an apple. He wanted her to talk for him, help explain his news. Well, she wouldn't. If he

wanted to be independent, let him! Besides, she kept pray-
ing that something might change his mind.

Uncle Voss was off on the Thanksgiving bonfire when
a motor stopped out front. In a minute steps sounded
on the porch, and Sammy recognized the quick, efficient
knock.

"Lee!" she said and ran to answer.

CHAPTER TWELVE

He stepped inside, smudged with grease and dirt. "The well
came in. No oil, but it's good pipeline gas, and it'll pay off."

Sammy didn't know whether congratulations or con-
dolences were in order. She decided that the safest course
was to bring the hot coffee he plainly needed. When she
came back with cups and a carafe, Lee was sitting on an old
leather stool, looking tired but relieved.

"The gas will keep me in business while I make some
more wells," he explained. "It isn't riches, but it's sure better
than a dry hole, which I was about to conclude we had. I
still think there's oil around that location."

"Where will you drill next?" Chuck asked eagerly.

Lee smiled his thanks for the coffee before he shrugged.
"Wish I knew. If I hit more gas, it'd be okay, but a dry hole
would sure set me back."

"Doodlebug has a site all picked out," Sammy chuckled.
"He'll be after you."

"You're not just whistlin' 'Dixie,' young lady! He jumped
me as soon as we saw we had gas. I'll take another look at
his spot to calm him down, but shucks! You use every test
you know to find the best place and then hit gas, if anything.
What would happen if you followed a peach twig?"

Looking into the golden flames, Sammy spoke dreamily,
"You might hear the dicky bird."

"I'm afraid his song is too expensive for me." Lee
grinned.

After a few minutes of oil talk, Uncle Voss rose. "C'mon,
Chuck. Lee's been on that well so steady he and Sammy
haven't had a chance to visit."

Tall and thin, moving alike, the two remaining Forrester

men passed through the door. Lee glanced in dismay at his soiled clothing.

"Doggone, this is nice of your uncle, but I'm so dirty I can't touch your little finger. In fact, I'm scared to even be in the house. I came right from the rig."

"Relax. We *live* here, you know." She poured him more coffee before she went to stand by the fire, hands crossed behind her. She had on his bracelets and they jingled with a merriment she wasn't feeling as she thought of her brother.

"Lee," she said, "don't hire Chuck. Please."

"Why not?"

Her jaw dropped. "Because he shouldn't quit school! I'm surprised at you, Lee, encouraging him to drop his education."

"Hold on." Lee set the cup in its saucer with a click. "I didn't encourage him to do anything. He said he'd quit school, that he was interested in oil, that he needed a job. My drunk tool-pusher is getting fired next time he shows in camp. I'm shifting the crew around to fill his place, and I've got a vacancy for a roughneck on the 'boll-weevil corner' where new men always start. If Chuck can fill it, he can have it."

And she had counted on Lee for backing! Sammy stared at him in disbelief. "I did tell Chuck not to feel bound if he decided any time he wanted to go back to college," Lee added. "He's trying to be a man, Sammy. He has to make up his own mind."

"If—if you think I'm going to like you any better for this—" she began, but Lee came to his feet, towering over her, and he said in no uncertain terms that he hired and fired and had been working in oil before she started third grade.

"That thought never entered my head, ma'am." His voice was rich with gentle sarcasm. "I never mix business with pleasure. I'll treat Chuck as I would any hand, neither more nor less. Get this, Sammy, *I* run my business."

Frantic to hit back at him, she grasped the bangles, jerked them off in a fierce motion that bruised her arm. "You can have these! I don't want them! I—I—darn you, I thought you'd help!" She started to whirl out of the room but Lee caught her and he didn't apologize this time for being dirty.

He kissed her. Not the way he had before, swiftly and light as if forcing himself to remember her age, but in a sure, hard fashion. When he stepped back, still holding her wrists, his eyes would have frightened Lupe and his voice was strange.

"What do we have to do with the rig, or whom I hire?" He put his hands far back on her cheeks so that his fingers slipped into her hair. "You're special to me, Sammy. Let's keep it that way. I have to run my business the way I see it." He put the bracelets in her hand and used the Spanish phrase. "But in other matters, *señorita, servidor de usted.*"

She laughed with some bitterness, though her flash of anger was gone. "I don't want you to serve me in other matters, Lee. But I guess you're right. Chuck's too big to hog-tie and ship forcibly back to A & M." To seal the peace she put on the bangles again.

Lee nodded. "Thanks. I've got to go now." As she stood forlornly by the fire, he tousled her hair. "Don't be so glum! Chuck may change his mind overnight."

That was almost what happened. Sammy came awake next morning to a knocking on her door. She slipped into her pajama coat and padded to answer. Chuck ducked inside like a criminal.

"Sam," he began, establishing himself on her study chair. "You've got to help me tell Uncle Voss. Sort of ease it over him. I tried last night and you heard him—on and on about dear old A & M. Now you've got a smoother way than I have, and——"

"And you want me to tell him?"

Chuck nodded. "Yes, sort of."

Sammy crossed to her mirror and sat down. Deliberately she began brushing her hair. Chuck hitched his seat closer, hunched forward with his elbows on his knees. "Aw, Sam! Don't make me suffer!"

"I'm just thinking." She put down the brush, eying him. "Telling Uncle Voss won't be the easiest thing in the world for me either. It ought to be worth something to you." Chuck stared as if this couldn't be his sister, his twin; they had always considered their property as immediately divisible by two.

"What do you want?" he asked in a stricken way.

Sammy giggled. "Well, not a pound of flesh. You can leave your shirt buttoned. I'll do your dirty work on one condition: That you go back to school and complete the semester, take your exams and such. Close the term out so that if you ever want to go to college, you'll have a few grade points."

"Why—why—that's blackmail! Downright blackmail!"

"True." Sammy blew on her fingertips and smiled. "And the black is getting darker every minute."

Chuck groaned. "All the women in the world and I get you for a sister!"

"Take it or leave it. I don't want that little chore one bit. You can surely stick out another three weeks."

After a moment of inner struggle Chuck sighed and got up. "Okay. I'm whipped. I'll finish the semester if you'll break the news easy to Uncle Voss—you conniver!"

"Chuck!" She turned him around from the door with her call. Going to him, she gripped his arms. "Please, why don't you tell Don about the boots, or go to Whit?"

"Run to my sister's boy friends?" Chuck wrested free. "Not much!"

"They'd give him a Cadet Court for this. Isn't that what you've been wanting all year?"

Chuck shook his cropped red hair. "Not this way, because of a private thing. I wanted to get him on some offense directed at the school in general. Otherwise, it's like having the Corps pay off a personal argument." Chuck's hands clenched. "I'll get him man-to-man if I get a chance—take those boots out of his hide. But I won't tattle-tale."

Who could understand men? Their odd sense of pride and honor? Sammy grimaced. "If this magnificent hair-splitting is the result of A & M indoctrination, it may be just as well you quit," she thrust.

But at the end of vacation she took him back to school. Privately she had resolved one thing. She wouldn't tell Uncle Voss till the ultimate, absolute last minute.

Maybe the news would leak out to Don or Whit and they'd discipline Ragan. Or, dubiously, Chuck might change his mind. There were three weeks yet. A lot could happen.

English school started again. Sammy was distracted from it by Chuck's trouble and the fact that Martín and the *vaqueros* had gone into the little hills after the coyote dun. They rode out, with extra horses, the second of January, and had been gone now three days. Sammy caught herself listening for hoofbeats, and whether she was in the house or in the English school she found herself constantly peering out the doors and windows toward the distance-misted hills.

Once they picked up the dun's trail, one man would dog him on horseback, while the others camped, the idea being to keep the wild horse on the move, without rest, while relays of a fresh horse and rider would relieve the tired ones. It wasn't necessary to hurry, keep the dun galloping or anything like that. He would be gradually "paced" down and lassoed when he was exhausted, or simply hazed into the corral.

Sammy tried not to think about that part. She'd be good to him, and there was no question but that he'd eat better from hay and oats than the sparse graze in the hills. He would sire fine colts and make Los Ladinos a proud name in horse circles again. Of course, he first had to be caught. So while she watched for signs of him or the *vaqueros,* she worked out a few new wrinkles in teaching.

Tomás had brought her a fine, large mud turtle and she had given it quarters in the school. The children thought him beautiful with his green and amber shell, and the way he poked his head in and out of his shell gave them plenty of excited practice in saying, "He's in his house! So-Slow is in his house." Or: "Look, Señorita Sam! So-Slow is coming out of his house!"

Sammy's best idea came from Lee. He had startled her one night by announcing gaily, "Win, lose, or draw, I ought to hear that dicky bird! We spudded in the Doodlebug Number One this morning. Right where the peach twig dipped."

"You're joking!"

"Nope. I couldn't find a place that looked especially promising, and Doodlebug kept wandering down the draw with that darn twig, all sad and mournful. His promised land looked as good as any, so I decided it was worth it just to restore his faith in the modern breed of oil men. Men go bust for a lot worse reasons than reaching for a dream."

He gazed at her so intently that Sammy had to look away. Up toward the hills were Martín and the men, chasing her dream—the spirit of Los Ladinos embodied in a dun with the black streak of the untamed ones down his spine.

"I hope the Doodlebug comes in and makes you a million, Lee. Did you get a man for Chuck's job?"

"Diego Ruiz's brother." Lee grinned. "I'm glad you got the kid to go back to school, Sammy. Chances are he'll stay." He wrinkled his nose appreciatively. "Say, what kind of perfume are you wearing?"

"Perfume?" Blankly, she glanced down at her dress for a clue, laughed as she saw a fine sprinkling of flour. "That's almond extract! I've been making cookies. Come in and have a few?"

"Since you twist my arm."

Inside, sharing warm cookies and milk with Uncle Voss, Lee returned to the almond extract. "It really did smell like some kind of Oriental perfume," he insisted. "I wonder if people realize how much pleasure they miss if they have a dulled sense of smell? That's the only thing I don't like about the oil business. You smell these gosh-awful odors till fainter, nicer ones can't be detected anymore." Munching on another cookie as if to console himself, he brandished a finger. "If I were a big wheel in education, I'd urge a course in Smells. Train the kids to recognize at least twenty or thirty scents."

"I'd back you," said Uncle Voss, fondly stoking his pipe. "Anything that gets people to live a little more keenly, experience their lives down beneath the eyes and skin, is a good thing."

"I can detect that pipe a hundred feet away on a windy day," Sammy charged. "Not being able to smell might be a good thing!" But she thought it over and came up with "sniff bottles."

They were soon the rage of the school. Pill bottles were filled with a bit of cotton dipped in some odoriferous solution—ammonia, salt, vinegar, gasoline, alcohol, rose water, lavender, vanilla, lemon, and so on. The children could take turns sniffing and see which one could identify the most samples. Sammy kept a score sheet. Each week the Champion Scent Detector was to get a package of fancy-shaped soap, footballs for boys, roses for girls.

Now that prepositions and some of the harder things were learned, Sammy could have more elaborate lessons, give the children practice in conversation that stretched further than the bare essentials. When she heard Rudi and Chuey rattling away in English, she felt a warm sense of accomplishment, of having done something useful. Her inner life had not been happy since fall, but it had helped to have the school and know that seventeen or eighteen young lives were off to a better start because of her.

At noon on the sixth day after the *vaqueros* rode out, Sammy heard the pulsing rage of hoofs, shouts, and the squealing of a furious horse from the corrals. She left the table half set and ran outside, sprinting for the mesquite enclosure.

Gathered around it, heads and shoulders visible through the fog of dust, were Martín, Jorge, and Comanche-blooded Vicente, who was shouting like one.

As the dust cleared, Sammy's eyes fastened to the beast in the corral, who raced about, heading pell-mell for the fence, shying away at the last instant. Dark mane and tail flying, he was the shade of a sun-warmed arroyo bank everywhere else except for the black coyote markings down his back.

Coming up by Martín's saddle, Sammy gripped his hand. "Martín, you got him! The coyote dun!"

"Yes, Señorita Sam. We paced him five days so that he neither rested nor grazed and now we bring him back to you."

The old *vaquero*, bent over his pommel, wore such a stern look that Sammy felt accused. Moving toward the corral, she leaned on the rough boughs. "Beauty, beauty," she spoke under her breath, even as a surge of pity for the caged wild one almost beat down her determination to own him. "You won't be sorry. You'll be king of Los Ladinos and someday you'll love me. And there'll be Chispa and the other horses to graze with and lean your head against."

To the younger men who had ridden up Sammy said, "A thousand thanks, my good friends. I know it was a long, hard chase. Each of you shall have one of the colts he sires. It is my hope that his get will breed back toward the old Los Ladinos mustangs. If this happens, perhaps we can quit raising watermelons. That should cheer even you, Martín."

The head *vaquero's* steel-gray brows tugged together. "What will be, will be. If you are pleased, that is enough." He inclined his head and rode away, followed by the men. Sammy moved back to the fence.

"You're mine," she told the dun, who kept circling the corral. "And I'll call you Mesteño for your blood, and because you're wild. Tonight, you drink and rest. In a few days I'll start getting you used to me."

"You'd better let Vicente work him first," came Uncle Voss' voice from behind her. Sammy whirled.

"Isn't he splendid?" she cried. Then what her uncle had said got though to her and she checked, frowning. "But I don't want Vicente to break him! I want to train him myself, right from the start. Otherwise he won't be mine."

Uncle Voss' gray eyes expressed something between amusement and worry. "You want to own things, don't you, Sam? You hate to let go. It can work like squeezin' a bar of soap too tight—shoots it right out of your hand."

Let go of things? Why should she?

In the bright sun Sammy returned her uncle's gaze, which seemed to judge her in spite of its love.

"Why should I let go?" she demanded. "Hasn't enough been yanked away?" Her old world, Mother and Dad; then Whit, her dreams of life with him. You bet she was going to hold on, and break Mesteño too! But her pleasure in watching the horse was blighted. She walked toward the house, not waiting on her uncle.

CHAPTER THIRTEEN

Sammy didn't want to go at Teño—as she came to call the coyote dun—so fast that he'd react permanently and violently against training. Besides, it was good to watch him as he cantered about the pasture or grazed on the knoll. The pride in him was almost tangible, like the wild, free spread of his mane and tail. After he had been in the pasture three days, Sammy saddled a gelding and rode out toward Teño, circling and urging him into the corral that opened into the small pasture.

Then she closed the gate. From behind it, she talked to the wild horse, accustoming him to her presence and her voice. After a week of this he stopped plunging and trying to escape the mesquite walls. He drank at the tank and licked the salt block, keeping an eye on Sammy though he seemed to have concluded that she was merely an annoyance, like a gnat that couldn't be eluded and so was best tolerated. Sammy decided to begin actual contact after Chuck's fate was settled. She didn't want to miss a day once she started gentling the dun, and if Chuck quit school she'd have to drive up and bring him home.

The semester was almost over. She hoped something had happened to change his mind. How *was* she going to tell Uncle Voss? He felt as if she and Chuck were his own children and had perhaps an even heavier sense of responsibility. If anything went wrong with them, he'd believe he had failed his dead brother as well as the twins. Lupe would take it hard too. She was so proud of Chuck.

As January wore on, Sammy grew tense as a fiddle string, only she couldn't tune herself up to speak. Finally, in despair, she thought that when the last hope of Chuck's sticking it out had vanished, she'd not try to camouflage or embroider; she'd simply say that Chuck was quitting.

On the Friday before final exams, she had a phone call. It was long distance, and she stiffened with terror and delight as she recognized the voice, once familiar, now so strange.

"Sammy," Whit said at once, his next words shattering her joyously confused imaginings, "do you know who brine-soaked your father's cadet boots?"

Fingers tightening on the phone, Sammy fought against the lump of disappointment and hurt blocking her throat. Her head buzzed. It was a few seconds before she could speak.

"Why don't you ask Chuck?"

"I did. He pulled the three wise monkeys of India on me. I've talked with Don and have a good idea, but I want confirmation before preferring charges."

If Ragan were punished, Chuck might stay in school. Sammy wavered. It was Chuck's decision, and he'd chosen not to tell. "I'm afraid you'll have to get your information up there," she said. "How did you get mixed up in this?"

"I was in the shoe shop where Chuck had taken them for renovation, and the owner showed me. He was real shook up, because he'd made those boots and he remembered your father." His voice roughened. "I won't have such stuff going on in my wing. This isn't a personal matter, Sammy, it's a question of decency and respect for the Corps. Did Ragan have anything to do with it?"

"I'm sorry, but I can't tell you."

"Can't?" he said grimly. "Or won't?"

He sounded so dictatorial, so arbitrary, that she fairly squeezed the phone. "I'm not in the Corps, Whit! If you can't see what's right under your nose, why expect me to?"

"Don't you want Chuck to have justice?"

"The sort you handed him at the Cadet Court?" Sammy jabbed bitterly. "You didn't call me then."

"Sammy, for the love of Mike——"

"Don't know him. Good-by." She clicked down the receiver.

Of course she wanted justice! She wanted Chuck to go on with college too. But she couldn't violate his sense of honor, ridiculous though it seemed to her. Still . . .

Whirling, she ran to seek out Uncle Voss and ask if she could drive up to A & M next morning. She couldn't tell Whit the facts without Chuck's permission, but she could certainly argue with her brother. Tell him that if he wanted vengeance, here it was, and if he didn't, why leave shcool?

She was at the Student Center by noon, and phoned Chuck's barrack to ask him to meet her for lunch. "What're you doing in town?" he demanded. Before she could answer, he zipped on, "Boy, wait'll I tell you what happened this morning! Stay right where you are, Sam, I'll be there in a minute!"

Eaten with curiosity, she paced the corridor, admiring the pictures that hung the length of it. Had Chuck thrown Ragan to the wolves after all? She was surprised at the violence with which she rejected the thought. Chuck had sounded happy, and he wouldn't have been had he informed on Ragan. She spun at quick steps behind her, moved toward Chuck and hugged him in one burst of emotion.

"Hey, hey!" He squirmed embarrassedly, brushing the tip of her ear. "I haven't just surfaced after ninety days in an atomic sub. But guess what did happen?"

"Ragan committed hara-kiri?"

"Not that weird, but almost!" Pulling her toward the cafeteria, Chuck emitted a glow of well-being. "Whit found out about the boots yesterday. He asked me what happened, but I wasn't going to squeal."

"I know. Whit phoned me."

Chuck stared. "He did? Gosh, you—you didn't——?"

"No. But it brought me up here to see what you brilliant Aggies were doing. Proceed."

"Well, Whit finally let me alone. I told him the boots had been soaked but I hadn't seen it done and therefore couldn't accuse anyone. I thought that would end it, but who do you think came to my room this morning and apologized?"

"Ragan, I hope!"

"Yes." Sobering, Chuck slid into the booth across from Sammy. "Whit was pretty sure it was Ragan so he went up to his room late last night and really laid it on, I guess. Ragan thought I'd ratted and was plenty sore till Whit told him I hadn't. So Ragan asked my pardon this morning— real stiff and soldierly, of course! And then he asked Whit to send him before a Cadet Court for punishment. Can you beat that?"

"No. That must be what makes the Corps a thing men never forget. Will the Court give him a rough penalty?"

"I doubt it. They'll respect the fact that he asked for punishment. We'll probably walk the Bull Ring together a good bit, though."

"All by the end of next week?"

Chuck frowned in puzzlement a second before he understood. "Gol-lee!" he grinned sheepishly, "you better tell Lee I won't be taking any jobs except summer ones for the next few years. Till I finish school." He added, brown eyes serious, "When are you going to marry him, Sam?"

"That's a good question—one I haven't given much thought to." Sammy held her brother's gaze with her own, proud and glad that he had cleared his first bad hurdle with credit. "Congratulations, sir."

"Thank you, ma'am." Chuck bowed low. "Now," he persisted, "I want to know what you're going to do!"

If I only knew! Sammy shrugged. "I still can't see the Air Force, and that delectable Mavis gal may have canceled out that choice anyway. Right now I have the English school and Teño to train, and Lee and I have fun. I just live as it comes and hope things will work out."

Chuck snorted. "Come off it, Sam! You're not the patient Griselda type. You may make it till summer, but if you and Whit are kaput, then what?"

"There's always college," Sammy said, more to evade him than anything else.

"You plan to major in bareback riding? In trick roping?" Chuck's eyes twinkled but his voice was warm as the current that flowed between them. Twins, bound close by tragedy, they were choosing their lives now, ways that would necessarily take them different routes. Yet Sammy felt they would always be able to sense each other's moods and, often, thoughts. She studied her hands.

"I don't have any burning wish for college, Chuck. But I am learning that I want more than the ranch and horses, I want a family and people to love. However, I won't marry unless I do love. So I may well wind up studying to be a teacher. I could work with the little pre-primer kids along the Rio and maybe between them and the mustangs I could be useful and reasonably happy."

"*Reasonably!* That's some way for a girl your age to talk!"

"Would you rather I put on sackcloth and wailed?"

"If you're so fond of kids, you should marry," Chuck grumbled. "I bet Lee would ask you if——"

"Hush!" said Sammy in alarm. "I like Lee far too much to marry him just for a home. I let you work out your battle with the Corps. Return the favor, okay?"

"Mmmf!" fizzled Chuck. He subsided into his steak and salad.

"I saw Don Stuart yesterday," Chuck began offhandedly. "He wanted to know if——"

Sammy laughed. "Don't start maneuvering men at me," she warned. "Don needs to be getting his true love lined up for the Ring Dance, and I'm not the one. Don't worry, Chuck. Alkali will poison the first worm that gnaws at my damask cheek."

"Whit's still going with Mavis," Chuck remarked, his gaze vigilant.

With an inward wince Sammy tilted her head and said coolly, "That's nice, they're a handsome couple." She finished her meal with dispatch and left for the ranch.

Sammy rode up Tigre Creek next day to tell Lee the good news about Chuck. The Doodlebug Number One, drilled over on Ruiz's land, had already encountered gas sands, and the going was rough, but Doodlebug, coming out to greet Sammy, looked as if he'd been lit up with an electric light bulb.

"This is gonna be it, Miss Sam," he chortled. "I can 'most hear that old dicky bird flappin' his wings!" He went on talking about the positiveness of his peach twig till Lee came up from the rig to join them.

"Hi!" Lee said. "I called yesterday but your uncle said you'd gone to College Station."

"Yes, I went up to see Chuck."

Lee shot her a wary glance. "Is that all you went for?"

"What do you mean?" asked Sammy, stiffening at his tone.

"Voss said that boy friend of yours called."

"Whit is wing commander. He heard about the boots being soaked and was trying to learn who did it."

"He had to phone down here for that?"

"Oh, don't be incredulous at me, Lee! I—I guess I don't want to talk to you after all!"

She turned, heading for Chispa, but Lee got in front of her. "Forgive me, Sammy-*Mula*. I just can't imagine a boy calling you over nothing more ulterior than pickled boots. What did you learn about Chuck?"

"He's staying. Ragan 'fessed up, after some grilling from Whit, and now Ragan and Chuck can keep each other company while they walk off demerits in the Bull Ring."

"You're really pleased, aren't you?" Lee asked.

Sammy heaved a deep sigh. "You can't imagine! It was up to me to tell Uncle Voss. I'd have rather met the firing squad."

Lee's hand closed over hers. "And Whit, did he tell you how he'd played peacemaker and got Chuck to stay in school?"

"Of course not! I never even saw him." Sammy tried to pull free. "What's the matter with you?" she cried in exasperation.

He let her go suddenly. "Thanks for coming by. I'll see you soon. Be careful with that coyote dun." He swung abruptly down the arroyo to the rig.

After she had unsaddled Chispa and turned her out to graze, Sammy studied Teño awhile and went into the house. Uncle Voss was reading a stock magazine before the fireplace, and she sank down on a footstool beside him.

He still didn't know all of Chuck's ordeal, just the part about the boots. Sammy thought that her twin's struggle was his private business and something he'd rather tell his uncle in his own way.

"Uncle Voss," she said, staring at the scuffed toe of one small boot, "whatever did you tell Lee about Whit's phone call? I came by the rig today and Lee behaved like—like——"

Tossing the magazine aside, Uncle Voss took his pipe from between his teeth and gazed at her. "How do you feel about Lee?"

"Why, I—I *like* him more than almost anybody."

"Love him?"

"No." Wishing she'd never begun this, Sammy got to her feet. "We have a lot of fun together, though, and I—I need him."

"A crying towel is mighty convenient, especially a nice, good-looking one like Lee. He deserves better than that, Sam."

Angry blood thrummed in her ears. "He doesn't have to go with me," she retorted. "He knows how I feel and he says he'll date anyone else he wants to, any time he feels like it."

Uncle Voss scoffed. "Do you think a man in love as much as Lee is with you would quit as long as he had a prayer? As long as he can see you, he will—because he can't help it. Only it's not pleasant and convenient for him, it's a necessity, a painful one." When Sammy started to protest, Uncle Voss raised a silencing hand. "Besides, you say you need him. There might come a day when you'd marry him because of that need, because he'd be glad to have you on any terms. And that would be a half-marriage, Sam. Lee giving and you taking."

"You seem to know a lot about it for a bachelor," Sammy couldn't help blurting.

"I do." Uncle Voss looked straight at Sammy. "I loved your mother. She knew me first, remember. Then after she and my brother quarreled, she dated me again. I knew she loved him, but I kept hoping. I didn't let her go till I plain had to. So I understand Lee's spot pretty well."

"He's not in love with me, Uncle Voss! He—he said he wanted to teach me some male psychology."

"He's done a lousy job of it then!" Uncle Voss snorted. "Put yourself in his shoes a minute. He can't stay away unless you make him. But if you did, after awhile he'd look around. He'd see another girl, one who'd love him. Maybe someone like Fran."

Sammy thrust her hands in her pockets. "He dated her once and can again. Golly, he can do what he wants to, I haven't put a hex on him! And he treats me like a kid half the time."

"That's a defense."

Sammy couldn't think of an argument, so she told her uncle she had to help Lupe with supper, and escaped to the kitchen.

The next week, each morning, she worked with Teño, first approaching him on foot, stopping when he ran away, standing still and talking till he calmed. She brought him apples and he finally took them from her hand, his eyes wary as he chewed the succulent morsel. Ordinarily, she was in a hurry to get an unbroken horse used to the saddle and bridle, but there must be no false steps with Teño. There was no other like him, and she fought down her impatience.

When he came to accept her presence, she brought out a hackamore, the simple strap halter that slips over a horse's head but has no bit or control on the mouth.

Martín was at the corral that morning. When he saw the hackamore, he said, "Permit me, *Señorita* Sam, to put that on the coyote dun."

"*Gracias*, Martín, but I am capable," replied Sammy, with a courtesy that matched the chief *vaquero's*.

Prodded by the knowledge that he was watching, Sammy eased up to Teño, holding out the apple. She talked to him, keeping the hackamore behind her back and moving to his left side. As soon as he took the apple, she slipped the halter over his ears. He jerked, trying to jar off the leather.

"Easy, boy, easy," Sammy murmured, stroking his neck. He fidgeted and rolled his eyes till the white showed, but when no further nuisance followed, he munched the apple.

Sammy talked to him about five minutes and removed the halter. He drew in its smell with a blast of his nostrils and lipped at it, then turned indifferently away, as if convinced it had no life of its own and wasn't worth his interest. After a few days of the halter Sammy took a bridle along. Vicente, mending harness as he sat in the barn door, stood up and walked with her.

"I do not wish Chuey's English teacher to get stomped, Señorita Sam. Let me adjust the bridle this first time."

"How do you know it's the first time?" Sammy demanded.

As Vicente flushed guiltily, she thought back. Remarka-

ble that one of the *vaqueros* had been either around the
barn or corral every day since she began gentling Teño.
Uncle Voss may not have suggested it, but he certainly
wouldn't object.

She had trained at least half a dozen colts, some of them
mighty recalcitrant. Didn't anyone give her credit for some
know-how? Still, mingled with and subduing her annoyance
was the glow of feeling valued, of knowing somebody cared
what happened to her.

"Oh, I can handle the bridle," she assured Vicente. But
when she laid it down to open the gate, he took it without
a word. Sammy frowned, but decided to put the halter on
first and then ask for the bridle.

After she had the halter on and Teño was standing quietly, she called to Vicente to bring the bridle.

"Only if I put it on," said the *vaquero* firmly. "A horse
fights the bit at first and you are not very big. If the dun
killed you, with what words should I go to your uncle?"

Vicente never spoke in idleness. Besides, what he said
was true. Teño could rear his head far above her reach and
strike her down with his front hoofs in the process.

" 'Sta bueno," Sammy gave in after a moment.

Bridle behind him, Vicente came toward the dun, talking
in Spanish. Sammy relinquished the halter and moved out
of Vicente's way. Vicente, following what he had explained
to Sammy was the way of his Comanche forebears when
they wished to tame an especially fine horse, caressed the
horse all over, talking softly. The horse trembled but didn't
rebel. At length, Vicente raised up the bridle and had no
trouble till he tried to fit the bit between the dun's teeth.

Squealing, Teño brought up his head, began to lash up
with his forefeet, but Vicente, earing him down with one
sinewy hand, deftly slipped the bit in place, buckled the
throat latch, and the dun was bridled. He tried to curvet
away, but Vicente brought him around with pressure on
the bit.

Obeying the steel on his tender mouth, Teño was furious
but baffled. For the first time he actually had a real check
upon him, and he didn't like it. But his attempts to take a
hunk out of Vicente's arm, or wheel and flee from it all got
him only the maddening, painful bite of the metal.

Vicente walked him around a few minutes till he restively

followed the bridle tug. "You may have him now," he told Sammy, giving her the reins.

She nodded her thanks and Vicente retired to the gate. Sammy stroked Teño's neck and shoulders, feeling an odd shame. She had beguiled him with words and apples and petting, till he now was acquainted with the rule of a bit.

"Hua, horse," she murmured, to comfort both of them. "Don't be afraid. We'll feed you corn and oats, *caballo,* and you'll like being rubbed and brushed. You'll love me as I love you. Come along, boy. Walk with me."

Keeping the pull as gentle and steady as possible, Sammy led him around the corral. He moved nervously, head out-thrust, lifting his feet reluctantly. Sammy took care to keep her feet out of the way of his. One colt she had broken had stepped on her foot, bruising it till it swelled blue and black and she limped for weeks.

She kept Teño moving for fifteen minutes, long enough to prove that nothing terrible would result from the bridle, but not long enough to goad him into a frenzied battle. When she took off the bridle and hackamore, he ducked his head between his front feet and tore off for the pasture, not stopping till he reached the place where he always lay down and rolled, clothing himself in fine dust.

"*Ay,*" said Vicente, as she passed through the gate, "he has lost much of his fear. When it is all gone, it will be easy to tame him, Señorita Sam."

"I hope so."

Yet as she took the bridle and halter to the barn, she wondered. Wasn't fear a natural protection against danger? Removal of fear, as when a coyote lost his dread of strange smells, could lead to death. When Teño lost all fear, he'd lose his freedom.

Part of her cried out against that. Yet to her he was Los Ladinos, the life she loved in a shape she could touch and possess. With his *puro español* blood, he was her dream of a proud breed to equal the old line of Los Ladinos.

Standing in the barn door, she looked out at him, and her will and heart fused in one resolve as she faced the sun and wind, breathing deep.

She would tame him, he would be hers. Out of this one desire she would not be cheated. He couldn't be both wild and hers, and so he must be tamed.

CHAPTER FOURTEEN

By Valentine's Day Teño was accepting the saddle blanket. Sammy whisked it off and on him till he ignored it. Next would come the saddle. When he was used to it, Sammy would ride him. Her blood raced at the thought and she quelled the sadness that somehow came with the idea of his final submission.

Out in the little hills, he would just roam around till he died. At the ranch he would never lack food, and have shelter from the bitter northers. That was the only sensible way to look at it.

For Valentine's Day she gave the school a surprise party. She and Lupe spent the whole morning making frosting for individual pink heart-shaped cakes. Pink lemonade and mint valentines completed the refreshments. Chuey led at playing the "Do you have—No, I do not have—" game with a red satin pincushion.

After some whispered conspiracy, Rudi announced that the children had valentines for both the *maestra* and Señorita Sam. With shouts and laughter the class descended upon them, bestowing hugs and mint- and cherry-flavored kisses.

"The best valentines of all," Sammy chuckled to Fran, who nodded wholeheartedly.

Lee came that evening after supper. Sammy brought coffee for him and Uncle Voss, and they sat companionably, their talk interspersed with the silences of people who enjoy each other's company even without conversation.

Coyotes howled from the little hills, one of them perhaps Loney. Sammy grinned at her uncle.

"Dreaming of summer and watermelons!"

He sent up a puff of fragrant smoke. "Yep. I've got to find her hangout. More than likely she'll have a litter of pups in the next month or so and I'd better get her before she has a whole pack of educated melon-eaters on me."

"There's a big white moon tonight," Lee said. "Maybe that's why they're howling."

"Whyever, they're sure singing," Uncle Voss said, and his

tone showed he enjoyed the weird, ululating chorus. "Has that dicky bird done any singing for you, Lee?"

With a wry grin Lee replied, "I'm afraid not. And we're down deep enough that I'm afraid the only song I'm fixin' to hear is 'Over the Hill to the Poorhouse.' Even Doodlebug's looking glum, poor old guy."

"Can't you move the rig to another location? I take it the operating expense is what has you hurting."

"I could." Lee stared into the fire. "For the same expense it'll take to drill this well to where it's hopeless, I could sink a fairly deep one in a new spot. I don't know." Shrugging, he stood up. "It's not cold out. Anyone care for a walk?"

"Not me," said Uncle Voss. "You kids run along. I'll sit here and think up plots to catch that durned Loney."

Sammy got her *rebozo* and they strolled out through the patio. The north winds had shaken off some of the older leaves from trees and flowering shrubs, but soon now the incredibly soft green fronds would force off the last old leaves. It was green all year in this country except when drought scorched things yellow; but there were a dozen shades of green and in the spring they were loveliest. Now moonlight silvered out the other shades. Sammy gazed toward the small fierce hills from which the coyote voices thinned and swelled. She was completely unprepared for Lee's question.

"Sammy. Am I poison that you can't love me?"

His tone was so light it took her a second to understand. Breath catching, she turned to face him, dismayed, shaken.

"Oh Lee, I——" His fingers pressed over her mouth.

"Wait. Listen all the way. I know Whit's still in your mind. But look!" His voice roughened. His big hand which had sustained her so often made an angry, impatient gesture, and he set his palms on the wall at either side of her, closing her in. "I want to scrap that bargain we made, Sammy. Try to put that cadet out of your head and give me a chance. I won't blame you if it doesn't work, but I want you to *try!*"

A pleasant fright stirred in Sammy, a feeling like the loss of balance as Lee kissed her. She felt the muscles of his arms tauten as if he were fighting to keep them on either side of, rather than around, her.

Shaken, Sammy brought up her hands. She didn't have to push. Lee moved back.

"I'm not sorry. I guess from now on, Sammy, you'll have to expect that."

Her voice stuck in her throat. Almost in panic, she said, "Maybe we shouldn't be together any more. Lee, I'm afraid——"

"Of what?" He laughed though a muscle twitched in his jaw, and his eyes were more than she could bear. "Listen, I love you! For six months I've watched you stew over that Whit and I'm through sitting on my hands."

"But I don't love you, I can't!"

"We'll see about that. I'm going to try my darndest to make you see me as I am anyhow. Then if it's still 'no', okay." He kissed her again, lightly. "Good night. Don't push the panic button, honey. I won't eat you alive."

For a long time after he was gone, Sammy looked out at the lonely hills and cried. Because Lee loved her, because she loved Whit, because life was such a muddle, and because the coyote dun grazed in the pasture and soon she must break him. She began to understand Diego Ruiz. To let go was the hardest thing in the world.

Uncle Voss came up to the house a few days later, holding two furry balls of yellow-gray. "Loney's pups," he explained. "I found them today in the little hills." Sammy cuddled one of them. It wriggled like a puppy. Its pink tongue licked her hand.

"Where's Loney?" she asked with an odd leap of regret. "Did you shoot her?"

"No. She finally landed in a trap, probably one of the neighbor's, and dragged it nearly all the way to where she had the pups stashed. She gnawed off one paw and started the next before she died. There must have been poison in the bait." Uncle Voss turned with the other pup in his arms. "Let's get some milk and feed these rascals."

Following, Sammy asked, "Are you going to try to raise them? Martín says it usually won't work. Their wild streak outs sooner or later."

"Reckon it might. More'n likely they'll be chicken-killers or eat melons like their mama." Uncle Voss stuck his finger playfully into his pup's ribs. "Still, Loney went through a lot to get back to them. I guess I owe them a chance, for that old melon-eatin' coyote's sake. I sure will miss her singin'."

Lupe clucked and scolded, but even she relented and smiled as the pups thrust their pointy tongues into the milk, found it good, and lapped faster, their lank little tummies, filling up as visibly as balloons. Sammy leaned down.

Wetting a finger with milk, she sprinkled a drop on each baby scavenger. "I christen you Rio," she told the runt. To the fatter, she intoned, "You shall be called Grande."

"*Grande* nuisance," warned Lupe. But she crumbled up corn bread and put it in the milk.

It was lucky for the pups that Uncle Voss found them when he did, for a norther blew in that night with drizzling rain and for three days South Texans shivered. The stinging, piercing wind made it colder than zero temperatures in other places. Sammy had to stop working with Teño till the rains stopped. She filled in the time by cleaning cupboards and making five pounds of assorted candy to mail to Chuck. His letters were still short, but they held a brashly confident note that said all was well with him and the Corps.

On the fourth morning after the norther the sun came up as bright and big as if it had never been hidden. Sammy spent ten minutes reminding Teño how the bridle and blanket felt. Then she tied him by the gate and brought up the saddle.

He skittered at the sight of it.

"Whoa, boy," Sammy wheedled. "Take it easy. You just stand still and———"

But he wouldn't. He kept moving and Sammy kept following. When he was standing parallel to the fence, she thought she had him. With the right stirrup and fender flipped over the seat so as not to bang down and startle him, Sammy hefted the saddle up.

She went sprawling as Teño's shoulder struck her; he bolted between her and the post. Instinctively rolling beyond the reach of his hoofs, Sammy collected her breath.

By the time she was up, brushing dust from her clothes, Martín and Vicente were in the corral. More wounded in her pride than anything, Sammy shook her head at their anxious queries.

"I'm fine. He doesn't like that saddle a bit though."

"It isn't hurt," Vicente said, after looking it over. "I will saddle him, Señorita Sam."

It was hard enough for her to hoist the thirty-eight-pound saddle on the back of a politely motionless horse. Sammy nodded.

"If you would do this as a favor, Vicente."

He had the iron in his wrist that Chuck had recommended, and he got Teño by the headstall, holding him, while the other corded hand swung the saddle in place. As the leather fenders and stirrups whacked down on his sides, Teño shrilled and fought, but Vicente kept his head down. Sammy closed in and tightened the cinch, but didn't force it snug enough for riding.

"Thanks, Vicente. I think I can take him now."

Vicente scowled. "He's mad. He has indignation. Do not work with him this day. Let me accustom him to the saddle."

"No, I thank you. He must obey me."

She held out her hand. Unwillingly, Vicente yielded up the reins. He and Martín didn't leave. They stood by the gate. Determined to show both them and the dun, Sammy kept a tight grip on the headstall and led him more by it than by the reins. If she let him get his head up, he was likely to thrash out at her with his forefeet or yank free, for the saddle infuriated him.

As they moved about the corral, Sammy stepping fast to avoid his hoofs, it was hard to tell which one was compelling whom. Sammy's arm ached from maintaining a steady drag on the headstall. She was glad to stop after ten minutes, lead Teño back to the post.

How, now, to get the saddle off? Sammy wished that Vicente would help, but after telling him that she could manage, she wouldn't ask for aid. She tied the reins to the post. Before she could get back to the cinch, Teño danced sideways, crowding against the fence again.

"Okay," Sammy breathed, "if that's how you want it!"

On guard this time, she stood as near the front of him as she could and still manipulate the cinch buckle. If he tried to highdive past the way he had before, she'd grab the bridle and either fight him back or get stomped.

Talking to him, she got the cinch undone. But she had to step back to drag off the saddle and he went through the space between her and the post.

Sammy, staggered by the sudden full weight of the saddle in her hands, stumbled back a few paces, but she wasn't hurt. She dumped the saddle at a safe distance and shifted around the prancing hind feet toward Teño's head, waving back the *vaqueros* who had run forward at the dun's charge.

"What's wrong with you?" she demanded, seizing the bridle. She brought his head down, smoothing his neck. "Why is the saddle so bad? Hmmm? You haven't been real onery, not till today. *Cuál es éste?* What is this?"

"He knows that to bear things on his back is to be a servant," said Martín somberly. "If he must be broken, Señorita Sam, let us do it. I think he will cause damage to someone before he is tamed."

Slipping the bridle off Teño, Sammy watched him make for his favorite rolling place. How beautiful he was! Worth taking pains with. Sammy turned to Martín with a smile.

"I'll ride him, old friend. Once he is used to the saddle, it will go well."

Only it didn't. The saddle wasn't simply a new, hence alarming, thing to Mesteño. For as the week passed, he resisted it just as violently as he had the first day.

Could it be what Martín said? Did the wild horse sense that once he submitted to the saddle, a rider came next? Each morning Sammy went and fought it out with the dun, permitting Vicente or Jorge to saddle him, but doing the rest alone.

"Do you have to do this?" Uncle Voss asked one noon when she came up from the corral, covered with dust and limping from being knocked down by one of Teño's lunges.

She laughed, spanking dust off her clothes. "I'm going to. I'd feel ashamed to ride a horse I hadn't been able to break."

Lupe scolded too, fueled by Martín's reports. "This is nonsense, Sammy-*Mula!* Girls are not given pretty bones to see if they can twist and snap them. You have a nice mare. Let this wild one go to the *vaqueros.*"

"Chispa has been bred to Teño. They should have a handsome colt. But Teño—I want him for mine, Lupe. In the fall I go to school. I'll learn to be a teacher, and I'll be grown up. Teño is the last gift I'll ask from the brushland."

"I do not want you to crack your neck, Sammy-*Mula!*"

"Let me rub yours, Lupe," Sammy smiled, resting her

friend's head on one palm while she massaged the aching muscles and nerves with her free hand. "Nothing bad will happen. And this is the first of March. Chuck will be home for Easter next month."

Lupe's eyes softened. *"Ay,* my Chuck! So pretty. For my birthday he sent me an A & M pennant and a fan of ivory." She brooded lovingly over his picture, still adorning the kitchen wall, and forgot Sammy's willfulness.

Kneading till the stiff bunches of muscles went soft, and Lupe sighed with content, Sammy went in to clear off the table. She had her hands full of dishes when somebody knocked.

"Come in," she invited, rushing back to the kitchen with her load. She re-entered the long front room as Doodlebug stepped through the door, pulling off his wool stocking cap that gave him the appearance of a sun-bronzed Santa Claus.

"Why, Doodlebug! What're you doing here this time of day?"

"I quit. Figgered you might put me up here, Miss Sam. I've saved my wages and I can pay board."

"You know very well you always worked enough to more than pay your keep," Sammy chided. "But—*quit*? Did you fall out with Lee?"

Doodlebug fretted the cap in his hands. "No, Miss Sam. Fact is, he don't know I quit, 'cause he'd have made a fuss over it." The old eyes peered into hers, fiercely bright. "Thing is, Lee don't think there's oil in the Doodlebug, and I'm havin' doubts. I think he'd like to try another location, only my bein' around bothers him. With me gone, he'll do what he figgers is his best chance." His shaggy white hair moved emphatically. "Lee's a good man, Miss Sam. I don't want him going broke because of me."

Sammy could have wept for Doodlebug. He was giving up what had sustained him all his wandering life, the belief in his power to divine oil, his hope of hearing the dicky bird again. And she knew he was doing it to free Lee, not because he, Doodlebug, wouldn't have given his life to see the well go all the way.

"You sit down and I'll bring you some coffee," she said. "Have you eaten?"

Doodlebug nodded. "I fed everybody good before I left, and I told one of the roughnecks to tell Lee I'd quit as soon as I had time to get well out of camp. I cooked a big ham and six pies today. By the time that's gone, Lee can find another cook."

Sammy went for the coffee. She wished Uncle Voss were here instead of at a meeting in Laredo. He could talk better with the old man, but she'd have to do her best.

"I think you have this figured wrong," she told Doodlebug, once he was sipping hot coffee and dunking vanilla wafers in it. "Lee told me he had no idea whether it'd be best to drill on or switch locations. He's a businessman. He isn't going to throw money away on purpose. Why don't you let me drive you back?"

"Nope. I can't anywise have it on my conscience, Miss Sam."

With variations, though she talked an hour, that was all Sammy could get out of him.

"Well," she said at last, giving up, "your old room is ready. Where are your things?"

"On the veranda. I didn't have much, so I carried it wrapped in an old slicker."

"You walked?"

"Sure. I don't have a car." He was crossing to the door when a car stopped in front. The steps weren't Uncle Voss', and Sammy ran to the door, flinging it open.

Lee stepped in. "Howdy. I'm looking for the best cook in Texas." His glance fell on Doodlebug. "And there he is! What do you mean by running out on me, oldtimer?"

"I'm in your way, Lee. Drill you a new well. I should of kept my mouth shut 'stead of talkin' up my peach twig's spot."

A crease formed between Lee's brows. "I didn't drill because of the twig, but because the indications were as good there as any place. The well's going on down whether you come or not. Now are you fixing to leave me without a cook?"

"Why, I——"

"I think it's pretty small of you to walk out on a camp of hungry men." Lee ranted, though his eyes twinkled. "I thought you'd try to do the right thing, Doodlebug, but you sure left me up a stump! Who's going to make breakfast?"

"Now, Lee——"

"Oh, if you can live with yourself after doing this to me, go right on," Lee interrupted. "I guess that old dicky bird was wasting his breath when he sang to you."

"Looky here, Lee, that's plenty!" Doodlebug rose, his jowls puffing. "I'll come back and cook for that sorry excuse of a crew, but don't you drill any deeper on my account!"

Lee chortled. "Throw your stuff in the car, oldtimer. The men'll be glad it's you cookin' their breakfast instead of the boll-weevil man."

A bit sheepishly Doodlebug told Sammy good-by and went out. Sammy caught Lee's arm.

"Did you intend to stay with this well?" she whispered.

Lee quirked an eyebrow. "I was about ready to switch. But when the old man took off to save my feelings—shucks, Sammy, it's only money. And oil is where you find it. We've still got a chance."

Sammy squeezed his big hand. "You know, you're pretty wonderful!" His mouth tugged down crookedly.

"Sure. That's what all my girls say. Good-by, Sam."

That night about eleven, the Doodlebug Number One came in, spewing oil over the men, the derrick, the earth, before it was brought under control.

"When the oil came in, I heard the dicky bird screech," vowed Doodlebug, who came with Lee before breakfast to break the news. "Just like it was Burkburnett and the early fields. Did you hear him, Lee?"

"I reckon I did." Lee's green eyes burned and his laughter echoed against the wall. "When that oil shot up, after all that time—why, I heard the dicky bird, and Gabriel blowing his horn and the Fourth of July and Christmas. It looks like a good well too. Ruiz will get enough from royalties to build him a town if he has a mind to. And I'll sink other wells. If we get a real field, it'll make jobs and help quite a bit around here."

Sammy looked at Doodlebug and her eyes stung. She was glad that for at least one more time he'd heard that great strange bird whom he'd followed all his life. And she was glad, oh very glad, that Lee had his well.

Spring was coming again, the early spring of south Texas, Lee had his well, Chuck would soon be home for Easter, and still Teño rebelled at the saddle. And each day, too, Sammy found it harder to go on with his training.

Any creature who willed to be free this much—wasn't it wrong to tame him? She ridiculed such feelings. Teño merely fought the saddle because he was skittish. Of what earthly use was it for him to spend his life in the mesquite thickets?

Grimly, she decided that this one thing she *would* do, no matter what. It was somehow mixed up with Whit, the fact that she hadn't been able to sway him. He had done exactly as he pleased. And now Mesteño wanted to go his way, but he wasn't going to.

This very day she would ride him. He couldn't fight a rider much more than he resisted the saddle. When she went to the barn for the riding gear, Vicente was rubbing the little horn "buttons" of a young calf with caustic potash to keep them from growing. He finished with the indignant baby, sent it bounding long-leggedly off, and helped Sammy lift down the saddle.

"You work the dun again today, Señorita Sam?"

"Today I'll ride him."

Vicente recoiled before his Indian impassivity masked his dismay. "I do not think you should do that. The spring has made him all wildness."

"It may be so," returned Sammy in Spanish. "But my brother will be home in two weeks. By then I wish to have Teño used to a rider."

"Con el favor de Dios," said Vicente, frowning, "with the favor of God, you may ride him. But why tempt heaven? Let me break the dun."

Sammy shook her head as they walked toward the corral. "If I cannot tame him, Vicente, I shall set him loose. Chispa will have his colt and with it, at least, we'll have one of the old line." She lifted her chin. "I'll ride him though. Don't you have belief in me, after you and Martín and Jorge taught me to ride?"

"It is not that you lack skill or courage." The *vaquero* was close to Sammy and the wind brought to her his odor of black tobacco and mesquite wood smoke. "A mustang is a mustang. And this one has the black spine streak of the coyote, the mark of the lone ones. I cannot prevent you, *Señorita* Sam, but I can stand near with my *reata*. That I may save you if you are thrown."

Sometimes *vaquero* fatalism could be downright unsettling. *"Gracias,"* said Sammy drily and passed through the gate. Vicente, carrying the saddle, followed as she approached *Mesteño,* who snuffed up his head from the watering tank.

His black mane and tail moved in the breeze. He shifted on his small ebony hoofs uneasily, for here they were back again, these beings with the hard things to set in his mouth and on his back. Sammy spoke to him, crooning.

"Ay, caballo, little horse. Stand still. You know me . . . Yes, this is how the bridle goes. *'Sta bueno?* Come on now, have your apple." She petted him as he crunched the offering, and gripped the headstall and reins as Vicente put on the saddle.

All her soft words and strokings couldn't reconcile the dun. She bore down on the leather straps with all her power, keeping the head down, for once he got it up, she couldn't control him at all. Vicente fastened the cinch and grasped the bridle, relieving her. Sammy stepped away, flexing her numb fingers.

Mesteño's neck arched so that the swelled muscles pulsed, hinting at the leashed fury inside him. He fought the men, dancing, trying to break that iron hold.

A chill of fear, so extreme that it shot through her like an electric shock, seemed to leave Sammy's mind separated from her body. She suddenly was not involved in this at all except as the puppet figure who was gripping the pommel, going into the saddle. But in spite of this detachment she breathed old Martín's prayer:

"En el Nombre de Dios!"

She was on the horse, she took the reins that Vicente yielded with his dark face tense. Teño's hoofs thrummed an infuriated tattoo, but the *vaquero's* steely hand kept the headstall until Sammy should be ready. She clamped her knees tight and took a long breath.

"Let him go, Vicente!"

The man released the bridle, made for the fence. Mesteño plunged after him, head thrust out, jolting, lashing out his rear legs. Sammy pulled on the bit, hugging the saddle with her legs, bent low over his neck, trying to turn him from Vicente.

Maddened at the bite of metal on his tender mouth, Teño swerved; lurching about, he stampeded to the other end of the corral. Checking at the barrier with a force that slammed Sammy's face into the pommel, the dun erupted into a fit of jackknifing crow-hops. A slow, warm seepage flowed from Sammy's nose over her benumbed lips. Her teeth clicked together and her spine felt cracked into little segments.

They were nearing the fence again. Sammy hauled on the bridle, throwing her weight and pulled sideways. She had to get him leveled out, send him into a circling run away from the barrier. But it was no good.

He was past responding to the steel in his mouth, past veering away from an obstacle. He must have been aware only of the hateful presence on his back.

Up he went, his front feet clearing the bars, but he had leaped too near his hurdle, and Sammy's frantic pressure on the bit impeded the jump. They struck the fence with a rending crash.

Sammy heard her own cry, and Vicente's, saw a flash of sky through splintering limbs and the bulk of Teño's body which seemed coming down right on top of her. She wrenched free of the stirrups and rolled just as something struck her head and everything went black. She must have lost consciousness for only a few seconds.

Rousing to Vicente's voice, his hands dragging her out of the wreckage, Sammy turned to see what had happened to Mesteño. The sight of him wiped out her sense of bruised, shaken pain. She pushed up to her knees.

He was trying to rise, but one leg wouldn't take his burden. He struggled and neighed, finally lurched up without the help of his right forefoot. It hung useless, the hoof touching with its tip on the ground.

Cold horror dazed Sammy. A broken leg was almost a death sentence for a horse. *Oh please — let it just be sprained*. She twisted away from Vicente's supporting hand, pleading.

"Vicente, look at him—can you see what's wrong?"

With deft, practiced fingers, the *vaquero* examined the leg, shook his head as he pointed to where swelling had already begun in the shoulder and the upper foreleg.

"His bone, I think it is broken here, Señorita Sam."

"But you're not sure! Maybe it's a bad sprain. Please, Vicente, take the pickup and go right now for the veterinarian."

"Had you not best go along and see the doctor? Perhaps the fall damaged you. Your face is bloody."

"Go!" Sammy almost shouted, beside herself with fear.

Vicente left, but she heard his tones over by the barn. He must be telling someone. She limped around and studied Mesteño.

His eyes were strange, glassy. He seemed unaware of her, as if his injury had taken him into some place where she and his surroundings no longer mattered. His crippled leg accused Sammy and she tried to think of a way to at least diminish his pain.

An ice pack? She hurried toward the house, was stopped by Martín as Vicente whizzed past in the pickup.

The chief *vaquero* had tears in his eyes. "Praise be the good God you live," he mumbled. "I will see to the dun. Have Lupe attend to you." Sammy ran on to the house, back to the storeroom. Besides her nose, which felt cracked, she was bruised and cut all over by the fall and the wood splintering down upon her. But that could wait, everything could wait, except Mesteño.

Lupe, dozing in her rocker, woke and screamed as, ice bag in one hand, Sammy yanked open the refrigerator.

"Sammy-*Mula*! Are you dead?"

"Of course not! But Mesteño's hurt. Please help me get this bag full of ice cubes."

"A plague seize that *maldito* horse!" Lupe stormed. "Your face it is ruined, perhaps you are crushed within! Now maybe even Señor McAllen will not love you. Whom shall you marry? Oh, I always said it! Whistling girls and crowing hens——"

"Don't, Lupe! Hold the pack while I fill it, will you?"

But Lupe, continuing her lament, had rushed out, to return with towels and alcohol and *Guadalupana* salve. While

Sammy stuffed the bag, Lupe washed her face, daubed it with alcohol and the salve.

"Your nose is puffed, *ay de mi*! But not broken, I think. Possibly, too, the cuts will not mark you. Your uncle is not here or he'd take you to the doctor. You must lie down and I will call the hospital to send someone out."

Sammy detoured Lupe's detaining hands. "I'm fine, truly! Don't worry." She sped through the house and across the grounds to the corral. Mesteño was as she left him. Martín glanced up, sighing.

"This is very bad. I think the bone is snapped in more than one place."

"You—you think he must be shot?" Sammy faltered.

Martín nodded. Tears coursed down his leathery cheeks, tears for this last wild one whom he had captured against his own wish. Sammy gulped, blindly pressed the ice pack on the dust- and sweat-stained shoulder.

She had caused this pain; there was nothing she could do to help it, and she writhed inwardly with guilt and regret. If things could just go back one hour—if she could have the choice again, to ride or let the horse go free . . .

But he stood here, patient and dulled beneath her hands, and that was the worst part.

Time faded as they stood there, she, Martín, and the coyote dun. Then, the station wagon following the pickup, Uncle Voss and Vicente and Dr. Barr arrived together. Uncle Voss drew Sammy to one side, his eyes full of the compassion he couldn't utter. It only took Dr. Barr a few minutes to go over Teño's leg, and turn to her.

"I'm sorry, Miss Forrester. He's snapped both his foreleg and his shoulder."

Uncle Voss' arm tightened around Sammy, but she moved away. "Dr. Barr, can't you splint it—do something?" The vet looked from her to the horse, pursing his mouth.

"I could fix him in a sling. But even if the leg healed, it'd probably break again when he started using it. In any case, he'd be crippled. He's yours, of course, and I'll try it if you insist."

Uncle Voss avoided her gaze. "We'll let you think it out, Sam." The men walked off. Sammy turned back to her horse.

A whitish film had covered most of his eyes. She put her arms around him and he permitted it. The life, the spirit, was out of him. It was like embracing a statue that could somehow suffer and sweat.

How could she condemn him to being crippled? Hadn't she wronged him enough without trapping his pride in a maimed body? She put her face against him and kept, tasting his sweat with her tears, both bitter salt. He had liked her voice and so she talked to him now, hoping that beneath his pain he'd feel how she felt. "Good-by, little horse. Good-by, *caballo*. Where you go now you'll always be free. There'll be sweet water and good grass. Forgive me—what I did. Good-by. I love you."

She went to her uncle who waited with the others at the gate and said, "Can you shoot him?"

Uncle Voss nodded. She walked mechanically to the house, to her room.

She never heard the shot, though her unwilling ears strained. Neither could she eat, though Uncle Voss brought a tray and said he'd called Fran to tell her the English school couldn't meet that day. Toward evening Sammy drowsed from sheer exhaustion, woke at the distant howl of a coyote.

Sitting upright, she thought for the first time of Mesteño as being dead. The buzzards and coyotes would feed on him unless she went out quickly and disposed of his body. She had better burn him, the way an animal with an infectious disease was handled.

"I shot him out by the oak thicket," Uncle Voss said in return to her question. "He died fast and without much pain. There's no use in your going out there, Sam," he added as she went down the porch steps.

"I'm going to burn him."

He set down his pipe. "Let me help. You'll need that big can of kerosene."

"Thanks, no. I'll do it myself."

With the big can bumping against her leg, Sammy cut through the corral, the small pasture, and moved toward the clump of dwarfed oaks. It was a silver-blue night, with a half-moon. Over in the little hills coyotes were still crying. She found Mesteño easily and began covering him with brush.

When she had a great heap about him, she threw on the kerosene and lit a match.

Flame zoomed up, casting forked tongues into the suddenly black sky. The smell of mesquite and salt cedar, tangy and stinging, covered any other odor. Sammy kept bringing up limbs and twigs. It took a long while. And all the time her mind asked the tormented question: *Why?*

Was it always going to be like this? Would everything she loved be snatched away? Her parents, their happy world; Whit; and now the coyote dun who was to her Los Ladinos, her golden place incarnate. She had loved, wanted, needed them all—and through her desperate fingers they'd slipped away.

Yes.

But in the glimmer of the mesquite fire she realized something. Mesteño had died because she'd tried to keep him, had insisted on his being hers. Some things died if you held them too long and too tight. Early love, maybe? A stubborn dream of a world exactly as you wished it without considering that the person you'd placed in that dream might have glimpsed another thing far beyond you—*Whit with his eyes turned to the clouds. How could she tie him to earth?* Only these thoughts couldn't turn the dark shape under the coals into a living Teño who'd run off wild to his little hills. She dragged up more wood. The flames mounted, whipped in the wind as Teño's mane had, and slowly, Sammy saw something else.

The coyote dun would never be broken now, never tamed, or ridden. He had died free. He'd never grow old and slick-toothed, avid for pasture. If he had lived, a cripple, it would have been agony for that spirit. In her heart Sammy would see him always running free on the hills, the elusive wildness of all the mustangs in him. Feeling this, she could at last let him go. And in that cleansing, freeing moment came her freedom too. The coyote dun was the life she'd wanted, Los Ladinos with Whit. Whit was many things. First love, good friend, a part of the refuge and happiness she'd found at Los Ladinos when her old life fell apart.

Deprived of the coyote dun, forced to look into her naked heart, Sammy discovered with slow wonder that she loved Whit as she did her past, as she did Teño, irretrievably gone. She wanted Whit because he was part of the old impossible dream—and if that was how it was, she didn't love him *now*. Now, he was a different person from the boy who had shared her past but had to make his own future.

142

How wise he'd been to suspect it and make them both wait! Stunned, Sammy knelt and waited till the fire burned to coals. Then she sprinkled sand on it and came away.

Lee was starting across the pasture as she came back. Uncle Voss must have told him about Teño, for he took the empty can and matched his step to hers.

"I'm sorry about the dun, Sammy. Are you all right?"

His voice gentled down the rising grief in her; she knew with a shock that he was the only person in the world she wanted to be with right then. How could such a big, rugged, experienced man be easier to talk to than even her twin?

"I'm just scratched."

"You'll heal." Lee's voice sounded strained. "I'm leaving for Corpus Christi tomorrow. There's a promising lease available."

"Oh no!" Sammy blurted, the cry rising out of her stripped emotions. "You—you can't!" Then she heard what she had said and swallowed, starting to apologize.

Lee stopped her. "I can't?" There was a quick eagerness in his tone. "Why not, Sammy?"

Why not indeed? When she had let go of Teño and Whit and her old dreams, why was it hard to say good-by to Lee?

"Why," she said, marveling, "I love you! I love *you*."

"Imagine that," Lee murmured, and she knew he was smiling.

He kissed her and held her close to him for the first long time, and Sammy understood what grown love was; when nothing or no one else would do—when the other person made all the world you could ever want. When Lee had said he was leaving, there hadn't been any question in her reaction. She wanted to be with him, wherever it was.

Holding her away, Lee spoke solemnly: "My work means a lot of moves too. It won't be easy for you. Of course most of my fields will be in this half of Texas, and maybe you can keep on with English schools in other places so you won't be bored when I'm gone. I know how you love the ranch, and I want you to be sure."

Sammy laughed brokenly. "Lee, I—I've been doing some making sure back of my brain all these months, it seems. I know I love you because there wasn't any choice about going with you—I *had* to, if you asked me. As long as it's our life together, I'll love it."

But self-doubt welled up in her. Lee was adult, wonderful, all she could want, ever. But what, really, did she have to offer him? She bit her lip, trying to be honest. Only tonight her stubbornness had killed the coyote dun.

"Lee, are you sure? I'm not anything yet! I feel so young and stupid and clumsy. How can you know how I'll turn out?"

"I know."

"How?"

His big hands cupped her face. "Look," he said patiently, "aside from the fact that I love you, your looks, your talk, your ways of moving, you happen to be one whale of a person. Didn't you start the English school right in the ruins of your hurt over Whit? Because your plans were all fouled up, did you take it out on the world? You are absolutely what I want and I've known it since you told me I hadn't lost my shirt!"

It was dark but Sammy felt as if a bright sun were flooding her. It felt so good to *know* after months of hesitation and blindness and looking back to a time that was gone as permanently as Diego's drowned city.

Lee said, "I still have to go to Corpus, but I can come back every week or so. Do you think by June you could get used to the idea of marrying me?"

Sammy reached up to kiss him. "It's a wonderful idea!" she said, "and I'll be quite used to it come June."

* 9 7 8 0 5 9 5 1 6 0 4 4 0 *